Sean Williams was born in the dry, flat lands of South Australia, and forty years later still lives there with his family. That hasn't stopped him becoming a number one *New York Times* bestselling author, with almost thirty novels and numerous short stories for adults and younger readers currently in print. A multiple recipient of both the Ditmar and Aurealis Awards, Sean is the author of *The Crooked Letter*, the first fantasy novel in the history of Australian speculative fiction to win both awards. He has also worked in the Doctor Who and Star Wars universes, the latest release being his novelisation of the computer game 'The Force Unleashed'.

Sean has written reviews, music (for which he won a Young Composer's Award in 1984), a stage play and the odd haiku. Occasionally he makes up new words. When not writing or sitting on committees, he likes to DJ and cook curries (but not at the same time). You can find more at his website: www.seanwilliams.com.

Books in this series:

THE
Scarecrow

Sean Williams

Angus&Robertson
An imprint of HarperCollins*Publishers*

Angus&Robertson
An imprint of HarperCollins*Publishers*, Australia

First published in Australia in 2009
by HarperCollins*Publishers* Australia Pty Ltd
ABN 36 009 913 517
www.harpercollins.com.au

HarperCollins*Publishers*
25 Ryde Road, Pymble, Sydney NSW 2073, Australia
31 View Road, Glenfield, Auckland 0627, New Zealand
1–A, Hamilton House, Connaught Place, New Delhi – 110 001, India
77–85 Fulham Palace Road, London W6 8JB, United Kingdom
2 Bloor Street East, 20th floor, Toronto, Ontario M4W 1A8, Canada
10 East 53rd Street, New York NY 10022, USA

National Library of Australia Cataloguing-in-publication data:

Williams, Sean.
The scarecrow / Sean Williams.
ISBN: 978 0 7322 8476 3 (pbk.)
Broken land
For secondary school age.
Fantasy fiction, Australian – Juvenile fiction.
A823.4

Cover and internal design by Natalie Winter
Cover images courtesy of Shutterstock
Map and illustration by Matt Stanton
Typeset in Sabon 11/15pt by HarperCollins Design Studio
Printed and bound in Australia by Griffin Press
60gsm Bulky Paperback used by HarperCollins*Publishers* is a natural,
recyclable product made from wood grown in a combination of sustainable
plantation and regrowth forests. It also contains up to a 20% portion of
recycled fibre. The manufacturing processes conform to the environmental
regulations in Tasmania, the place of manufacture.

6 5 4 3 2 1   09 10 11 12

For George Watt, my first teacher

Contents

The Scarecrow's Island

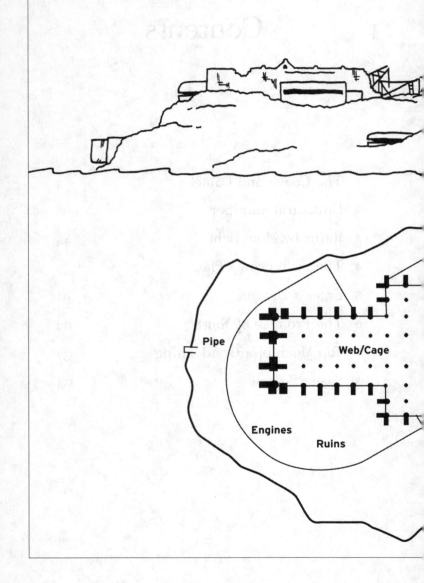

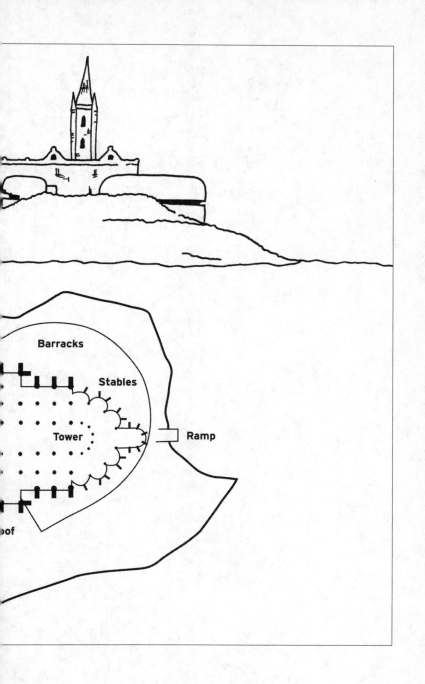

Barracks

Stables

Tower

Ramp

oof

Previously . . .

At the urging of his invisible friend, Escher, Ros runs away from his family and the drought-stricken farm where he has lived his entire life. While he and Escher are on the run, he meets a talking statue called Vasoph and the Stone Mage Dylis Shurven; together they give him a heart-name, Paril. He also befriends a girl his age, Adi, who is captured and killed by spider-like crabblers. Using the Change, a magical power that Escher describes as 'the energy of life', Ros brings Adi back from the dead, but her mind and body are accidentally split in two again shortly after. Haunted by her ghost, he returns home to confront the evil Golem of Omus, who has been masquerading as his friend Escher in order to ruin his life.

Ros cleverly traps the golem by giving it a heart-name too, and is released from its curse. But he cannot stay at home. He has lessons to learn and wrongs to right — foremost among them putting Adi's mind back into her body before she is lost forever.

His search for Adi's family, the Clan Sabatino, leads him deep into the northern deserts, where he falls foul of sand bandits and dust devils but finds an unexpected ally: a young Dunetowner called Yury. Together, Yury and Ros rescue Yury's and Adi's loved ones from the sand bandits, and track the Bee Witch to her lair. The ancient witch, a skilled Change-worker, has stolen Adi's empty body and plans to live in it herself. Quick thinking on Ros's part ensures that Adi gets her body back and the Bee Witch is destroyed.

Ros would like nothing more than to join Adi's Clan and live a quiet life, but he has one very important mission left to perform. The Golem of Omus is only trapped, not dead. Ros has promised to drop the crystal that is its prison into the ocean and thereby remove it from human knowledge. With his camel, Know-it-All, and the help of the Clan, Ros sets out to accomplish this last deed, so he can be truly free.

THE
Scarecrow

1

The Coach and Camel

Somewhere between Chemaly and Smerdon, Ros suspected they had become lost.

Adi, as always, disagreed. 'How could we be lost? There's only one road, and we're on it.'

That was true. The way they followed was made of hard, compacted earth, crushed into stone by centuries of horses, camels and wagons. It wound through a landscape of hills and waist-high grass, punctuated by angular trees and deep, steep-sided creek beds. There were few turn-offs, and they always led no further than the nearest farmhouse or paddock. Occasionally Ros spotted a lone worker checking fences or tending machinery. Such glimpses made him think of his home far away, the baked-dry fields of Mount Geheb, and the family he had left behind. This region, the Strand, was much greener than the Interior. Things grew here without struggle.

'We'll be in Samimi before nightfall,' said Varis. The Clansman rode his horse, Leda, with loose-hipped ease. 'That I promise you.'

'See?' Adi poked Ros in the back. 'Stop being such a worry-wart.'

Ros felt that they had a lot to worry about, but if Varis reckoned they were on the right track, then that would have to do. The Clansman had fifteen years' experience on them, and had been trusted by Adi's father to keep them safe. Such trust didn't come lightly.

Know-it-All snorted beneath him as though backing up Adi's rebuke. Ros reached down and patted the camel's flank.

'I just want to sleep in a proper bed for once,' he said to cover his unease. 'My back is breaking from so many nights on the ground.'

'Working for the Clan has made you soft,' Adi said. 'We should've pushed you harder.'

'Harder? You try cooking for forty people three times a day. It's no picnic.'

'And I had it easy?'

'I'd trade inventory and sums for scrubbing pans any time.'

'No, you wouldn't. And don't tell me you don't cheat every now and again. I've seen you at it.'

He flushed. It was true: sometimes he did call on the Change to make his chores a little easier — drying dishes or making the camp stove cook a little faster. Why wouldn't he, since he had the gift of it? He didn't like to advertise the fact, though, and he certainly didn't like talking about it openly.

The clopping of horse and camel on the hard road surface was the only sound as they wound across a low valley and up the far side. At the top, Ros hoped to gain a glimpse of their destination: Samimi, a large town where Clan Sabatino had connections with a salt trader and other merchants. That was the pretext for the trio's journey: Adi would negotiate her first deal for the Clan with Ros to assist her and Varis to protect her. That was how Adi's father had justified it to himself and the other Sabatinos, who had lost their favourite daughter once before. The truth was, they were there on Ros's mission first and foremost.

Ros gripped the leather pouch at his side, where the Golem of Omus rested in his crystal prison. As always, he could feel nothing of the creature's presence, although surely the golem must be raging in his cage, hungry for freedom.

From the top of the hill there was nothing visible but another hill — and, much further south, a faint blue haze that grew deeper with every hour.

Ros resigned himself to travelling a little further. He was only impatient because his journey's end was getting so close. There was an ache in his bones and heart that had nothing to do with sleeping on the roadside. He longed to be free of the burden that he had carried for so long.

Adi rocked in the saddle behind him, swaying as he did with every step the camel took. If she sensed his frustration, she offered no reassurance. She didn't need to. For all their disagreements, this was one journey he was glad he didn't have to take alone.

Varis was true to his word. The sun had barely touched the western horizon when they reached the outskirts of

Samimi. The town didn't announce itself — there was no wall or gate as Ros had seen elsewhere. Samimi made itself known by degrees, first by a house or two hugging the road, then by a caravan stop where several trading families congregated, preparing a fire for the night's communal meal. Other roads joined theirs, and soon the sound of voices was louder in the dusk than the birds calling to each other over rooftops.

Ros felt a familiar nervousness creep over him at being around people again. As much as he had been anticipating their arrival, he greatly preferred the road to any kind of crowd.

The atmosphere of Samimi was thick with smoke and cooking smells, and behind it all a spicy, exotic tang he couldn't immediately identify. Dogs barked at the coming night, and cats skulked along fences. A baby's cry caught Ros's ear from far away. There were families in Samimi. People lived ordinary lives here. Towns like this one were what most people thought of as normal.

'Wait here,' said Varis, dismounting and handing Adi the reins. 'I'll find us a room.'

He left them waiting at a crossroads that sported no fewer than three two-storey inns. A steady stream of dark-skinned people flowed by, on foot or by any other means available, including camel, horse-drawn cart, and even a strange wheeled contraption that propelled itself with a terrible racket up the centre of the street. Ros had never seen anything like it. Neither strand beast nor tractor, it possessed two glowing lamps that cast beams of white light into the thickening gloom. As it passed, Ros felt a tingle of the Change rush through him. Whatever it was, its engine ran on more than just alcohol.

Behind him, he heard Adi unwrapping the pouch her father had given her.

'Tally Wiskins,' she read from the instructions within. 'That's who we're looking for.'

'She with the salt. We'll ask around tomorrow.'

'She has connections offshore,' Adi said, 'so she should be able to help both of us.'

Ros nodded, thinking of the blue haze to the south that was no longer visible from Samimi's built-up streets. The sea was something he had only ever heard about before. He was keen to see it with his own eyes but in less of a hurry to venture out on it. Only the knowledge that a boat was the best way to reach the deep ocean convinced him that he should risk it.

Varis came out of one inn and moved on to the next. His cool gaze took in the street and his charges with one sweep. Ros wondered how they looked to others' eyes: two unattended young travellers, one light-skinned, one dark with white-streaked hair, riding a camel heavily loaded with baggage and leading a horse similarly burdened. Their clothes were dusty but fine — much finer than any Ros had ever owned before, thanks to the generosity of the Clan. The two of them had clearly travelled far and seen much. How much, he hoped the people of Samimi would never know.

Varis appeared again and, after making sure they were still safe, entered the third inn. Adi leaned against Ros's back. He didn't mind taking her weight. He had grown in recent weeks: hard work for the Clan had both strengthened and lengthened him. The ache in his back and legs was at least partly from growing pains, not just sleeping on the hard ground.

'Who are we this time?' Adi asked, her voice muffled by his shoulder.

He thought quickly, taking the letters of their heart-names and shuffling them using the cipher Vasoph the man'kin had given him in Jakati. 'Paril' led to 'Sovan', a name he had used as an alias before. Adi's heart-name, 'Jelena', took some more thought.

'Hakamu,' he said. 'That's your name today.'

'Nice.' She shifted slightly against him. 'Sovan and Hakamu.'

'And Varis.'

'Yes. Him too.'

Ros rubbed absently at one of the bee-sting scars on his right wrist until the Clansman returned.

'The Exchange has the best rooms,' Varis said, 'but the Coach and Camel has the better rate. Which do you prefer?'

'I like the name of the Coach and Camel,' said Ros.

'And I like the rate,' said Adi, straightening in the saddle.

'Then we're agreed.' Varis took back Leda's reins and patted her muscular flank. 'Let's get settled. The evening meal starts in half an hour.'

Ros's stomach rumbled at the thought. He was a much better chef now than he had been when he'd first run away from home, but he always relished the chance to let other people do the cooking.

They stabled Know-it-All and Leda at the back of the inn, where several other beasts were already grazing, then took their luggage inside and deposited it in a long but narrow upstairs room. It contained nothing but three sagging cots and the air was musty, but to Ros it seemed like luxury. There was enough room for him to stretch out, and a working indoor toilet just up the hall.

'This is the life,' he said with a grin.

'Easily pleased, you,' said Adi. 'I'm hoping there's a bath.'

'You smell okay.'

'I wasn't talking about me.' She returned his smile with white teeth gleaming. 'I'll suffocate if I have to stay in here a minute longer.'

Ros felt his mood lightening as the three of them headed downstairs. The interior of the Coach and Camel was bigger than any eating-house they had seen since leaving the Clan on the road to Moombin over a week earlier. The smell of food filled his head and he could barely contain his impatience as Varis arranged for them to join the small group gathered at long wooden benches to eat. They looked like a mix of traders and official travellers, all men bar one small woman in the blue robes of an official from the Haunted City. Ros had learnt very little about the Strand since crossing the Divide, but he knew the name of the capital and he knew how to tell the difference between a Sky Warden and an ordinary functionary. Anyone wearing a glass collar was bound to be strong in the Change and best avoided. This woman seemed unthreatening, but he kept an eye on her all the same.

The meal came, a simple but tasty broth of white-fleshed fish and soft green vegetables, with baked grain rolls on separate plates. Bowls of butter and salt were passed between everyone. Strand cooking lacked many of the spices Ros had become accustomed to using with the Clan, but was much more adventurous than anything cooked at Mount Geheb. He didn't share Adi's disdain for food that failed to make her eyes water.

There was a map of the Strand stretching across two whole walls of the eating hall. Ros idly studied it while he ate, noting the names. Samimi was marked with an arrow towards the middle of the long, unbroken coastline.

'Do you think you'll do it here?' Adi asked, following the direction of his gaze.

'I don't know,' he said. 'Maybe, if it's safe.'

'Safe for who? You or Escher?'

They could speak openly knowing that no one would recognise the former name of the Golem of Omus.

'Safe for everyone,' he said. 'What if he got out? It would be a disaster.'

'Nothing's going to happen to him at the bottom of the ocean. And the sooner he's gone the better, I say.'

'So you can get on with your mission?'

She shrugged and dipped a crust of bread into the broth. 'This isn't a holiday, you know.'

'I do know that. You want to prove yourself to your father, and I want to help you. I just —'

He stopped as the chef emerged with a bowl of leftovers and put it down on the next table along.

'I just want seconds,' he said instead of what he had been intending to say, which was that sometimes he was afraid of finishing what he had started.

As Ros returned to his seat with bowl replenished, the inn's front door creaked open, admitting a strikingly tall man with a curling grey beard. He carried a light pack and wore a close-fitting cap, which he removed immediately, liberating a mane that matched his beard. After exchanging a private sentence or two with the innkeeper, he shrugged out of the pack and came to join the others.

'My thanks, but no,' he told the chef on being offered a dinner bowl. 'Ale is sufficient. Your finest, please, and in pewter if you have it.' His voice was liquid and easy on the ear. To the room he said, 'I hope you don't mind my joining you while you eat.'

A murmur of assent encouraged him to find a space. The table at which Ros, Adi and Varis were seated was the closest. He settled himself next to Ros and smoothed down his clothes, raising a faint odour of smoke and mule. 'It was my intention to reach Bohm before full night,' he said, smiling his thanks for the mug of ale when it arrived. 'My steed is ailing, however, and the day crept away from me. So here I linger, grateful for the chance to enjoy civilised company a little longer. You are travellers too, I presume?'

Ros would have preferred to avoid conversation, but doing so would attract more attention than putting up with it.

'We're from Showell,' he said, picking a name at random from the map.

'But originally from the north, yes?' The question was directed at all three of them. Although darker than Ros, Varis and Adi were lighter in colour than anyone else in the room, marking them as foreigners. Instantly, the man waved the question away, as though sensing that he was being intrusive. 'No matter. I ask only because I have cousins in Yamarna. Distant cousins, not worthy of the family name. You wouldn't have heard of them.'

He looked despondently into his ale and Ros felt bad for being rude. Offering his hand, and ignoring Varis's surreptitious head-shake, he said, 'I'm Sovan, and this is Hakamu and her uncle, Varis.'

Adi nodded hello, although she too looked more cautious than welcoming. Varis ate silently, acknowledging their companion with only his eyes.

'Welcome to you,' said the tall man, 'from Arden Quirk.' He patted his chest, which made a faint jingling sound, as though he was wearing a mail undershirt. 'This is a fine town for visiting, which I'm sure its residents will tell you, although it's drier and browner than normal thanks to a lack of rain. Not far from here is the Well of Yunda, where you'll find a hole in the ground no bigger than you are from which a giant lizard supposedly burrowed to eat a flock of sheep. While you're there, don't miss the Proclamation Tree. It may be drooping a little now, but Gerd Yunda himself stood in its shadow, 'tis said, and declared the town to be his.'

There followed a long and amiable description of Samimi's attractions, which seemed far from impressive the way Quirk told them. Ros nodded politely and offered nothing, letting the man ramble on while they worked their way through the meal. A one-sided conversation with a harmless old crank would hurt no one.

It took him off guard, then, when the conversation suddenly shifted.

'You've travelled further than anyone else in this room, I dare say.' Quirk gestured indifferently at the others seated at the tables. 'You've seen more and heard more still. Perhaps you could attest to the veracity of a tale that's reached my ears from distant parts — a tale I can scarcely believe, for all that it comes with an assurance of utter truth.'

Ros froze in the act of swallowing his last scrap of bread. 'What tale?'

Quirk's eyes were sparkling and full of intelligence. 'How the Golem of Omus has been vanquished by a new hero from the north: Roslin of Geheb, a Change-worker born a humble farmhand but now so powerful he makes the mightiest Stone Mages look like amateur illusionists.' The man's voice rose to fill the entire room. 'Not satisfied with defeating one of the world's oldest enemies, he single-handedly took on dust devils, a Bandit King and the dreadful Bee Witch, and as an aside rescued an imprisoned Desert Queen from a fate much worse than death.' People were looking up from their meals, and Ros quailed inside, knowing what was coming next. 'Before he could be thanked, he rode off into the desert on his trusty camel, accompanied only by the Clan Princess he loves and whose life he has saved twice already. Have you not heard of him?'

Ros was still frozen with a lump of dead food in his throat. Adi was flushing furiously, unable to meet anyone's eye. It was Varis who answered, speaking for the first time in Quirk's presence.

'We've heard the tale,' said the Clansman whose name was unknown outside his own family. 'Surely it is a fancy, nothing more.'

'The story is said to originate with the heir of the Desert Queen himself, who befriended Roslin of Geheb in the desert. Could he be wrong? And the people who sing from Ulum to Mayr of the hero's strength and honour, are they wrong too?'

'If not wrong,' said the Clansman, 'then at least exaggerating wildly.'

At that, Quirk nodded. 'Yes. That is the nature of such tales. But a kernel of truth likely exists.'

'Many young men ride trusty camels. That much truth, and no more.'

Quirk nodded thoughtfully and stroked his beard. 'A camel he earned in the first of his many adventures, they say, given to him by a trader he defeated in a battle of wits.'

At that, a stocky man seated by the empty fireplace snorted and rose to his feet.

'You don't believe either?' Quirk asked him, clearly annoyed by the interruption.

'I have no appetite for lies.' With that, the man strode out the front door, shutting it with a loud bang behind him.

Quirk turned back to Varis with a raised eyebrow, his composure quickly restored. 'Exaggerations, fancies or lies? Perhaps we will never know. There is no harm in enjoying the tale regardless. It passes the time.'

The man garnered enough agreement from his audience to convince him to continue. He called for more ale and launched into a detailed telling of Ros's adventures. His voice was rolling and hypnotic, but Ros was far from soothed. His hand gripped the leather pouch at his side. He wished that he was a thousand kilometres away, and that the friends he'd made in the deeper desert had tighter lips.

From deep in his memory came the voice of Yury, the so-called 'heir of the Desert Queen', saying 'You need to lighten up a little'. That might be true; Ros knew he took things very seriously. But there was nothing wrong with that. It was in his character, ingrained by his life's experiences. The things he had done had been forced upon him; he hadn't sought them out or pursued them for selfish ends. Taking the camel, for instance, had been an act of desperation, not a stunt to show how clever he was. Fear had driven him, not bravery, and guilt still haunted him over some of the other things he had done.

If anyone was worthy of acclaim, it was Varis, who had protected them in a thousand small ways during their journey, and protected them now by standing and making excuses for them, saying they were tired and needed to retire ahead of an early start the next morning.

Ros felt Quirk's gaze on him as they left, but the man's recitation didn't falter in the slightest. He had reached the encounter with the crabbler coven, one of the darkest and most terrible experiences of Ros's life. In Quirk's version it became a jolly underground adventure, with monsters fleeing at the very sight of him. No one knew how awful it had been, except Escher, the golem who had lied to him.

As they climbed the stairs to the first floor, he felt Adi's hand reaching for his. He squeezed it, grateful for the comfort she offered and knowing that it went both ways.

Adi used the communal bathroom first and on her return urged him to do the same. There wasn't a bath, just a ewer of rust-coloured spring water, a bar of hard, yellow soap and several grey cloths. He scrubbed as best he could, scouring days' worth of dust from every pore and at the same time trying his best to scour away his annoyance at Yury. It wasn't Yury's fault everyone now knew Ros's name. People liked stories, and no one had told Yury to keep any secrets. That Yury was a well-reader and able to communicate with others like him all across the Interior hadn't helped.

When Ros returned to the room, feeling pink-skinned and goose-pimpled from the cool night air, he found Adi already in bed and Varis nowhere to be seen.

'Gone to check the stables,' she said when he asked.

Ros felt guilty for not saying good night to Know-it-All but excused himself for being distracted by Quirk. He knew he shouldn't be upset. The man hadn't meant anything by telling the story.

'We'll look for Tally Wiskins tomorrow,' he said, taking the middle cot so Varis could be closest to the door, as he preferred. 'Then we'll get rid of Escher so you can do your thing. I don't want to get in the way.'

The room was lit by a single candle, and by its flickering light Adi's dark face was barely visible. Her long hair was pinned and covered with a cotton net so it wouldn't tangle during the night. The streak of white curled like a letter in a long-forgotten alphabet.

'You're not in the way, Ros. I wouldn't be here at all if it wasn't for you.'

Her eyes glittered at him and he knew what she was thinking. *Have you decided what you're going to do afterwards?* That was the question hanging between them. The Clan had brought him this far so he could dispose of his captive golem. When that was over, what would he do with his hard-won freedom? Would he return with Adi to the Clan, and the requirement that he'd have to marry in order to truly belong? He feared that he might easily become bored with counting money and making deals, let alone cooking for forty people a day, but what was the alternative? Would he find a new road to travel? Would Adi be willing to come with him if he didn't go back to the Clan?

He was exhausted by deep thoughts and uncertainties. All he wanted to do was sleep.

'A la nana mi rey,' he sang, thinking a lullaby might put them both to sleep before they argued again. 'A la nana mi ro.'

'That song,' Adi said, sitting up. 'My mother used to sing it. Where did you hear it?'

The tune froze in his throat. Why had he chosen that particular lullaby? The answer came to him immediately: because it was familiar to her; because she had given him the memory of it herself, when he had needed comfort and strength in the deep desert during his first encounter with the dust devils. But he couldn't tell her that. She had been a ghost at the time, and she had no memory of those days. She was more likely to think he had stolen the memory from her, and from there it was only a short thought to wonder if he had stolen her heart-name, too. She thought she had freely given him her most precious secret, when in fact Escher had beaten her to it. It was better that she never knew the truth than that she misunderstood and became suspicious of him.

Before Ros could find a convincing lie, Varis returned. The Clansman looked worried.

'There was someone poking around the stables,' he said.

'Who?' Ros asked, remembering how closely Quirk had watched them leave during the story.

'He ate with us tonight,' the Clansman said, stripping off his overclothes and lying down on his cot. 'The man with no appetite for lies. I checked with the innkeeper and he has no beast to be stabled, so I cleared him out and waited to see if he came back. He didn't.'

Ros remembered the stocky man but could see no obvious explanation for his strange behaviour beyond that he was a horse thief, looking for an opportunity. If so, he would go disappointed in the Coach and Camel. The stables would be watched more closely that night.

'I'll sleep now,' Varis said, 'and check again in a couple of hours. Would you like the candle left burning?'

Both Ros and Adi shook their heads.

Adi slid deep under the covers and pulled the sheet right up over her head. The tang of wick smoke filled the room. Ros let it carry him to unconsciousness, lulled by the sound of his companions' breathing.

Distantly he remembered a riddle Yury had told him when they had parted on the edge of distant Dunetown. 'When you stop and look, you can always see me. If you try to touch, you cannot feel me. I cannot move, but as you near me, I will move away from you. What am I?'

The answer was *the horizon*. Ros often remembered that riddle when trying to get to sleep. In the desert or on the plains, the horizon was visible in all directions. Destinations came slowly, seen far in advance. Among the hills of the Strand, however, he could see barely a kilometre. The world could end just over the next rise and he would never know. Sometimes it seemed that the end of his journey was as untouchable as the horizon — but he was here now, in Samimi, and both dreams and success were not far away.

Ros woke in the middle of the night when he heard Varis get up, but he remembered what the Clansman had said about checking the stables and went immediately back to sleep.

2

Unnatural Slumber

Ros dreamed that a voice was calling him, slowly but insistently, using words he could not understand. He wanted to answer the call, but his lips were strangely numb — and so they still seemed when he awoke. The name the voice had used was Roslin, rather than Ros or Paril. *Roslin of Geheb.* He seemed to remember hearing the voice before, in other dreams, but he always forgot about them later.

Ros sat up with that blurry remembrance already slipping away from his mind and rubbed his aching legs. A trickle of sunlight formed a pool on the wall opposite the window. By its yellow glare, he saw Varis's bed empty and Adi still asleep. He tried saying 'Good morning' and the words emerged perfectly fine. She didn't wake, which surprised him. Normally she was up before him and telling him to stop being so lazy. Sleeping off the ground was obviously doing her good.

He said 'Good morning' again, a little louder. She murmured something sleep-blurred and irritable, and he decided to leave her a while longer. Feeling like an old man with aching joints, he stood and dressed, then went to the bathroom.

Wherever Varis had got to, he wasn't there. Ros washed his face and cleaned his teeth, hoping there might be bacon for breakfast. He couldn't smell any, though, so he wasn't hopeful. In fact, he thought, sniffing the air, he couldn't smell any cooking at all. That surprised him too. The sun's brightness suggested a time well after dawn. The inn's many travellers should have started breakfasting ages ago, ahead of their early starts. No one lingered when the road was calling.

Curious, Ros descended the stairs and found the inn utterly deserted. The tables and bar were unattended. The kitchen was empty. He touched the stove and found it merely warm from the previous day's fire. The chef should have had it burning hours earlier. What could have held him up?

From the crossroads outside came the sound of ordinary industry. People chattered and animals called as though nothing was amiss. Going to the main door, Ros found it locked and the key missing. He returned to the kitchen, tried the back door, and it opened just fine.

His anxious feeling remained. Something was clearly very wrong, and he was the only one unaffected.

He ran back up the stairs to their room and shook Adi until she finally opened her eyes.

'What . . .?' She blinked up at him in a daze. 'What's the hurry?'

'Don't go back to sleep,' he said, then rushed out of the room and began banging on all the doors in the inn. 'Wake up!' he shouted. 'Wake up!'

From the occupied rooms came a chorus of groans and curses. Some trailed off into mumbles, as though unconsciousness was returning already.

Remembering something he had once heard about the best way to clear a crowded room, Ros changed tack and yelled 'Fire! Fire!' Within seconds, doors were banging open and the inn's baggy-eyed patrons were stumbling forth, dressed in robes, underwear or sheets wrapped hastily around their middles.

Adi was one of them. 'Ros, what are you doing?'

'Come with me.' Ignoring a growing babble of confusion and accusations, he led the disoriented throng down the stairs to see what he had discovered. 'This isn't natural,' he said. 'Someone knocked us out during the night. If I hadn't woken up, we might have slept all day.'

'Why did you wake?' asked one of the inn's patrons.

Ros didn't want to give the most likely answer — because he was strong in the Change — so he turned the question back on the questioner. 'Wouldn't it be better to ask why someone did this to us?'

'Check the till,' suggested another patron, but that turned up nothing. The inn's contents appeared to be untouched, also.

'I'll check the stables,' said Adi, hurrying out the back door.

'Look at this,' someone called out.

At one corner of the bar, a series of markings had been drawn on the stone floor around an intricate device of ceramic and metal. The device was smoke-blackened and dead, but Ros could tell from a tingle in the air that it had once been thick with the Change.

'Has anyone seen a charm like it before?' asked the man who had found it, to a chorus of *no*s. He poked it with a stick and a large section crumbled into ash.

Ros was surprised to recognise the stocky man Varis had seen in the stables the previous night. Varis had been suspicious of him, but if the charm before them was evidence of foul play, why would the man have let himself be caught in his own trap?

Adi returned, breathless. 'He's gone,' she said. 'Ros, he's gone!'

Both Ros and the man with the stick looked up. The charm was forgotten as the stocky man hurried past Adi to see for himself.

Ros urged her with his eyes to calm down. They weren't supposed to be using their real names, no matter the emergency. 'Who, Hakamu?'

She realised her mistake but wouldn't be calmed. 'Varis! He's not in the stables. He's not anywhere. Something's happened to him!'

Ros felt his own concern growing. Varis was their protector; he wouldn't leave them alone for so long without good reason. If he wasn't in the inn or the stables, where could he be?

The man Varis had been suspicious of returned. 'He's still there. I don't know what you're talking about.'

The three of them hurried back to the stables. Ros was beginning to feel dizzy with all the to-ing and fro-ing, but a hope that Adi had been mistaken more than made up for that. That hope was dashed when they found the stables empty of anything but the usual beasts of burden.

'What are you talking about?' asked Adi, rounding on the man with dark eyes flashing. 'Varis was never here, and you knew it.'

'Varis?' His confusion seemed genuine. 'I thought you were talking about the camel.'

Know-it-All looked agitated, presumably by all the shouting. Ros reassured him with a pat to his nose. 'What does it matter to you?' he asked the man.

The man ran a hand through his wispy brown hair. 'Nothing. I'm sorry, I misunderstood. This is ... this is as confusing for me as it is for you. Can you think of any reason why your uncle would have left you here?'

He asked the question of Adi, who shook her head defiantly, looking as though she might burst into tears. That unnerved Ros more than anything. He had never thought to see Adi cry.

He opened his mouth to say something, anything, but stopped before a single word came out. He had just noticed something.

There were eight stalls in the stables. One was open. He crossed to it and sniffed the air. *Mule.*

'Do you know who else isn't here, apart from Varis?' he said. 'That man who told the stories last night. Quirk's mule is gone, and so is he.'

'He's taken Varis with him?' Adi's confusion was only deepening. 'Why would he do that?'

'He thinks Varis is Roslin of Geheb.' The man was staring at Ros with an intense expression. 'Your friend does look more the part, you have to admit.'

Ros flushed. So the man had heard Adi use his real

name. 'Don't tell anyone who we are. No one can know, or else —'

'Or else something like this might happen.' The man nodded. 'I understand. You should get out of here quickly, before he realises his mistake and comes back.'

'What if you're wrong?' Adi asked. 'What if it's Varis who comes back and we're not here?'

'I know Quirk. I never thought he'd stoop so low as theft and kidnap, otherwise I would've warned everyone about him. He always gets what he wants, and he obviously set that knock-out charm to get a head start.'

'We only have your word for all this,' said Adi, looking more flustered than ever. 'How do we know we can believe you?'

Ros could only stare at both of them, unsure what to do with the unasked-for advice. Varis would have known, but he was nowhere to be found. Should they fear this stranger or accept his help?

Know-it-All kicked at his stall, as though urging them to hurry.

The man seemed to come to a decision of his own. 'My name is Manton. I was born around these parts but am no stranger to the roads of the north. I've met roadies like you before and I know what it means to offer my assistance in a time of need, one traveller to another.'

Adi straightened. 'You follow the old ways?'

'I traded with Clan Kourakis for a time. They call me a true friend.'

The claim had the effect of calming Adi immediately. The old ways were a code of honour followed by all the

Clans, and true friends, like Ros was to Clan Sabatino, could be relied upon under any circumstances. Varis might be gone, but Manton was offering an unexpected security in his place.

Know-it-All kicked the stall again.

'All right,' Adi said. 'We'll believe you. But where do we go? We have to get Varis back, and we've no idea where Quirk has taken him.'

'I can help you with that,' said Manton. 'Wait here. I'll go back to the inn and retrieve all our gear. Be ready to leave when I get back.'

Before they could say anything, he swept out of the stables, moving surprisingly quickly for a man of his build. Ros and Adi were left speechless by the sudden turn of events. Ros felt that the world was spinning entirely too quickly, and he was sure it had nothing to do with side effects of the knock-out charm.

Adi was the first to move. 'We should do as he says.' She went to the stall containing Varis's horse and gathered his saddle and gear. 'Manton can ride Leda. If we move fast, we might be able to catch up with Quirk. He's only got a mule and he'll be carrying Varis as well. It's lucky you woke us up when you did, Ros. Ros? Are you listening?'

He heard his voice as though it came from far away. 'I don't understand. Why would Quirk want to kidnap me? What have I done to him?'

'He thinks you're some kind of hero. Goodness knows why.'

'But what difference does that make? What could he possibly *want*?'

Her head poked out of the stall. 'I don't know, Ros, and if you stand there scratching your head all day we'll never find out.'

She had a point. He forced himself to move.

Know-it-All nudged him as he opened the stall and began getting him ready for the road. The familiar ritual and the smell of the camel's rough hide reassured him in a way that Adi's words could not. There was a music to the jingling of harness and buckles that spoke to him more deeply than words. He and Adi may have lost Varis, but hope remained — assuming Manton was true to his word ...

Know-it-All bared his teeth at Ros's frown, but he couldn't help being suspicious. Ros didn't share Adi's automatic acceptance of the old ways. He himself had exploited her Clan's faith in those ways when he had met them on the road with Escher. It was possible that Manton was lying, or at least not telling them the whole truth. He didn't owe them anything, and they couldn't possibly have anything he wanted. Ros promised himself to keep an eye on the man even as they accepted his advice and assistance.

Both Leda and Know-it-All were ready when Manton returned heavily laden with packs and bedrolls. He had Varis's as well as theirs and his own, and his broad face was pink with exertion.

'Load up,' he said. 'We'll have to move quickly. The others have roused the innkeeper and her husband. When the authorities arrive and people start wondering where you've got to, there will be questions you won't want to answer.'

Ros did as he was told but couldn't help wondering. 'Why don't we go to the authorities ourselves? They could help us look for Varis.'

'They're bureaucrats and book-keepers. They'll want statements and investigations and all manner of forms filled in, and even then they won't believe you. You won't be able to prove you're not who you are, and word will spread. When Quirk comes back, he'll find you tucked in some sheriff's office, ripe for the picking.'

That wasn't a pretty picture. 'Okay.' Ros strapped his and Adi's packs to Know-it-All and helped Manton with Varis's and his own gear. Leda's hooves danced on the cobbles as she assumed the extra burden. When everything was stowed, Manton did a strange thing. Holding the horse's jaw in one hand, he took a moment to explain to her in even, soothing tones that his expectation to be carried was only a temporary one, and that she would be returned to her master as soon as possible. That settled her, and had a calming effect on all of them, even Know-it-All.

'Thank you,' said Adi.

'Save the thanks for later,' Manton said, swinging fluidly into the saddle. His well-worn leather strides creased perfectly to accommodate Leda's girth. 'Let's find your friend.'

Clicking his tongue, he spurred Leda out into the bright morning sunlight. Know-it-All followed of his own accord. All Ros had to do was go along for the ride.

* * *

It was a very different journey from that of the previous day, with a whole new set of anxieties. Manton hurried them down one of the arms of the crossroads parallel to the coastline, blending smoothly into the traffic with only a quick glance behind him to make sure they were keeping up.

Ros glanced over his shoulder in turn. A small crowd had gathered around the Coach and Camel's main entrance: sheriffs and tenants arguing about what might have happened to them overnight.

'I hope Varis paid,' he said to Adi.

'He did. We always settle in advance.'

Ros hadn't known that. Money was her field of expertise, not his. He allowed himself to feel relief that at least the sheriffs wouldn't come after them for failure to honour their bill, even if they had other suspicions.

Samimi grew denser and busier around them. They rode through a vegetable market, and passed rows of blacksmiths, leather-workers, tailors and surgeons, all hawking their trades. They came within smelling distance of several fragrant kitchens, reminding Ros that they hadn't had breakfast. The occasional sheriff and blue-robed functionary stood out from the crowd, prompting undue anxiety each time. Ros knew, though, that they shouldn't be the ones hiding from the law. Quirk was the criminal, not them.

An image of Varis trussed up like a pig and tossed over the mule's back haunted him as they hurried along. It was Ros's fault their protector had been kidnapped; Ros's actions that had led to an innocent man being caught up in something he wasn't part of. That gnawed at his conscience. He had to save the Clansman from whatever fate awaited him, for both their sakes.

A thought occurred to him: what if Quirk wanted 'Roslin of Geheb' for reasons that weren't sinister at all? What if he just wanted help defeating some terrible enemy?

But there were better ways of getting help, which didn't involve knock-out charms and kidnap. He could have asked directly, for starters.

And then what? Ros knew he would have said 'no' no matter how great Quirk's need. He had other obligations, like getting rid of Escher and helping Adi find Tally Wiskins, first of all. Perhaps Quirk had guessed that.

Adi sat as stiff as a post behind him. Ros wondered what thoughts were going through her mind, but was afraid to ask.

They came to a wide space with public water pumps and shaded rest areas. The sky above was perfectly blue and perfectly empty, apart from a single bird circling far overhead. They stopped to refresh Leda and Know-it-All, and Ros hurried to buy the three of them something to eat. A vendor was offering meat and vegetable wraps with a creamy garlic sauce. He took four, knowing that one wouldn't be enough for him.

Adi and Manton were deep in conversation when he got back. Having full mouths only slowed them down slightly.

'To be honest, I'm guessing,' Manton said. 'Quirk has a reputation. He moves through the towns seeking certain items, and he pays well, but where his money comes from no one actually knows. He never sells anything, as far as I've heard. He just buys.'

'What kind of things?' Adi asked.

'Junk, mainly. Scraps from the old times. Manuscripts and maps. Machines that don't work any more. Blueprints.' Manton shrugged. 'It's hard to say what will interest him.'

'Have you sold to him?'

'I have, twice. The second time, I was curious enough to follow him. He headed west from Samimi, following the coastal road. I stayed well back so he wouldn't see me. I swear he didn't know I was there. But then he left the road and I lost him. There were no villages or homesteads nearby where he could've hidden. He must have used a charm of some kind, because I never found him or his trail. He had completely vanished.'

'And that's where you're taking us?' Adi said. 'To where you lost him?'

Manton nodded around a mouthful.

'What if he took a boat? Or what if he went in a different direction entirely?'

'I could track him to make sure,' said Ros. He hadn't thought of this back at the stables; the need for flight had been so great that it had pushed all other possibilities from his mind. 'I sat next to him. I even shook his hand.'

'Tracking Varis would make more sense,' Adi said.

Manton looked cautiously optimistic. 'If it were possible, you could save us a great deal of trouble.'

'I'll need somewhere I can concentrate.' Ros looked around. 'It's too noisy here.'

'It's noisy everywhere,' said Adi, screwing up her nose.

'I know somewhere we can go,' said Manton. 'Let's get moving.'

They mounted up and rode out, warm now the sun had passed noon. Ros fished a hat from his pack and pressed it down firmly over his curly hair. Adi had let her hair loose and it streamed behind her as the camel loped quickly onward.

Manton led them off the main road and through a series of winding streets. The buildings pressed in closer and taller around them. They were entering an older, stonier part of the town. Commercial houses — lawyers, banks and accountants among them — took the place of shops and merchants. Doors were shut and windows rimed with darkness. The sound of their passage echoed coldly from the stark, forbidding façades.

They turned a corner and found themselves facing a steep hill covered with hundreds of thin, rectangular stone columns. An iron fence separated the hill from the buildings around it. Plants overran every available space, except where narrow paths had been carefully cleared across the hillside. As they got nearer, Ros could see names and dates carved into the stone columns.

Manton had brought them to a cemetery.

'You asked for somewhere quiet,' Adi said, and indeed the background noise of the city was noticeably ebbing as they approached the memorials to the dead.

Ros told himself not to be squeamish. Then he spied furtive movement among the plinths. Stone eyes blinked at him. Rocky limbs waved.

'Man'kin,' he said. 'There are man'kin here.'

'Only little ones, bought to maintain particular gravestones,' said Manton, pulling Leda to a halt by the gate. He dismounted and tied her to a fencepost. 'Their feet are bound to the monuments. If you don't get within reach, they won't trouble you.'

Ros tried to ignore the tiny animated statues as he dismounted and helped Adi down after him. The only sound the man'kin made was the scratching of limbs against stone. If they had voices, they didn't use them.

Manton led them to a covered area towards the rear of the graveyard. There were three wooden benches in its circular shadow, facing outwards.

'Is this suitable?'

'It'll do,' Ros said.

'How do you know this place?' Adi asked.

'My grandmother's memorial is in here. Come on, I'll show you.'

As Adi and Manton walked away, Ros chose one of the benches and sat on it with his legs crossed. It didn't matter how he sat, as long as he was comfortable. He needed to concentrate in order to remember everything he could about the person he was seeking. Varis was self-contained and private, and his conversation had always been about things relating to Ros and Adi. But Ros remembered little things, the things that mattered most. The way he sang to Leda when he brushed her down each night; the pattern of black hairs on the back of his neck; the smell of his sweat after a hard day's ride. Ros concentrated on those things and sent his mind out into the world in search of him.

The Change was impossible to describe. It flowed through him like water and at the same time lifted him up like the wings of a bird. It burned like fire when it had to, but it could also move invisibly, with the stealth of thought itself. He had cast his words across the land and changed the world just by wishing it, and he had changed himself in subtle ways by doing so. He had learnt in the desert that the Change came from all around him — from the bedrock and the earth — but it also came from inside him. When he drew too deeply on his strength, his nose bled, or he lost his voice, or his head throbbed with a hum so loud and painful it threatened to smother him completely. He instinctively knew there was a limit, and he had no desire to find out what might happen if he tested it.

Manton had said that Quirk had gone west, so he sent the focus of his charm that way, scouring the Strand for any hint of Varis and his captor. Their spoor was very faint, but he found it in the end, confirming that in this regard at least Manton was telling the truth. He pursued it further west even as it seemed to wriggle out of his grip. Quirk had disguised himself somehow, as he had disguised himself from Manton the last time. The man hadn't seemed strong in the Change at all when they had shaken hands, but he had a curious ability with it nonetheless.

Ros reached further and further, tasting rather than seeing the coastline as he went. Quirk must have travelled most of the night to have got so far. Just as Ros was beginning to think that the trail may be a fake one, designed to lead him far off course, it kinked suddenly to the south and stopped. He received impressions of salt and rock and water in vast quantities. Then something hard and metallic lashed out at his mind, like a sharp, iron beak, and pecked him away.

'Ow!'

Adi was instantly at his side. 'What did you see?'

He waved her away before his concentration completely dissolved. Again he tried to get closer to the end of Quirk's journey and again he was painfully rebuffed. It was like stubbing his toe combined with a toothache right between his eyes. His mind felt so bruised he didn't dare risk a third attempt.

When he opened his eyes, he saw stars.

'Are you all right?'

He focused with some difficulty on Adi, who was crouched before him, staring at his face with worry in her eyes.

'I'm okay,' he said. 'And I'm sure I know where Quirk is. It's just as you said, Manton. He's to the west, right on the coast. When I tried to find Varis there, something blocked me. A charm of some kind.' He rubbed at the bridge of his nose. The pain was imaginary, but it still felt as though his skull had been whacked by one of his sister's well-aimed stones. 'That means we're going in the right direction.'

'Good.' Manton nodded, although he too looked concerned. 'Are you well enough to ride?'

'Yes.' Ros stood on wobbly legs and almost immediately lost his balance. Something small and heavy had run up Adi's back and jumped from her shoulder to his. He whirled around, trying to get a good look at it. It seemed to be an animal of some kind, but its touch was as cold as stone. 'What ...?'

Adi reached out and caught the thing about its middle. 'One of those miniature man'kin followed us down,' she said, holding it up by a leg. It was a small stone woman, squirming and wriggling and flapping two tiny wings behind its back. 'Manton's grandmother's monument has been damaged. We found this running around free.'

Ros looked at it more closely. The man'kin twisted around to peer back at him and then resumed trying to escape. Its frantic movements were almost too fast to be seen. Realising that Adi's grip could not be broken, it reached up and pinched her. She gasped and let go. It dropped to the ground with a thud.

Ros half-expected it to shatter into pieces, but instead it made for Manton. He tried to dodge away but it caught his foot, climbed hand over hand up his clothes and took purchase on his shoulder. There, the whirring of its wings slowed, and it hunched low to avoid being forcibly removed.

'It acts like it knows you,' Adi said.

'I guess it does,' Ros said. 'Do you visit your grandmother's grave very often?'

Manton looked trapped. 'Often enough.'

'Enough to recognise you as family. It's yours, I'd say.'

'But I don't want it.' The man'kin scurried behind Manton's neck to avoid his grasping hands.

'I think you're stuck with it,' Adi laughed. 'With her, I mean.'

The tiny stone face broke into a smile.

'I think she understands us,' Adi said, leaning closer. 'Can you talk? What's your name?'

The man'kin looked from Adi to Ros as though they were trying to trick her, then she ran down Manton's body to the ground, where she wrote a word in perfectly executed, if funereal, calligraphy.

B R O N H I L L

'That was my grandmother's name,' said Manton.

'Makes sense.' Adi's eyes tracked the man'kin as she scurried back to her perch on his shoulder. 'It's the only name she's ever known, and she's tended it for . . . how long?'

Manton looked gloomy. 'Twenty-two years.'

'Then I'd say she's earned it. Bronhill,' Adi said, and the tiny wings whirred with pleasure. 'It's a nice name.'

A breeze sighed through the cemetery, making the plants rustle. Ros looked up. A bird was circling far overhead, lazily turning and wheeling as though looking for prey. He shivered, remembering that he had seen such a bird earlier that day, when they had stopped to water their rides. The more he studied it, the less certain he became that it was a bird at all.

'Come on,' he said. 'I feel like I'm being watched.'

Adi stopped trying to stroke the little man'kin's head and her expression became serious. 'Do you think someone's following us?'

'I don't see how they could be,' said Manton. 'No one saw us leave the inn, and we'd know if there was someone else here.'

Despite his words, Manton looked unsettled. They went back to Leda and Know-it-All, Bronhill riding high on Manton's shoulder with a hand on his ear for balance. As they passed through the gate, she didn't look back. Ros didn't blame her. It couldn't have been a happy life, watching the tombstones of the dead, unable to speak. He only hoped her new life would be better.

They rode hard the rest of the day, abandoning stealth and sticking to major thoroughfares that led out of the town's heart and into its extensive coastal sprawl. There seemed to be no end to it. In the desert, towns expanded in circles, except where mountains or ravines got in the way. On the coast, towns were stretched out like melted cheese so that more people could be near the water. Ros had yet to glimpse more than a blue blur through a break in buildings, trees and hills. He realised he could smell it, though. The tang he had failed to identify a day earlier was salt, mainly, and the things that lived in briny water. Living or dead, they smelled like nothing he had ever smelt before.

Gradually the town faded around them in a backwards replay of their arrival the day before. Spaces between buildings increased. Scrub crowded the road's edge. As the sun sank lower in the western horizon, birds became increasingly restive, squawking at each other as they fought over choice morsels. People hurried home before dark or sought other lodgings. Ros, Adi and Manton were among a small minority pressing onward into the dusk with no intention of stopping.

Sunset came and went with an explosion of colours. Soon the stars were coming out behind them and the last crimson sliver of sky was fading ahead. Adi hugged Ros tightly to stave off the chill night air, her fingers linked firmly in front of his chest. He was grateful for her warmth. The camel's plodding feet drummed out a rhythm beneath them in counterpoint to Leda's steady lope. He cast his mind forward, along the path Quirk had set for them, and found the point at which the man had left the road. It was probably less than an hour ahead. Tentatively he explored south of that point, and this time found nothing. No metallic pecking. No sudden pain. Nothing at all.

That only made him more certain they were heading in the right direction. Nowhere in the world was there *nothing*.

So when they took the southern turn off the road and reached the coast, Ros was surprised to find just the sea, the cliff and the moon.

They came to a halt right on the cliff's edge, moving carefully in case they stepped wrongly out of tiredness. Dismounting, they allowed Leda and Know-it-All to catch their wind and took in the view. The cliff stretched from left to right, as sheer as though a knife had been sliced through the land. Rippling like a snake, it seemed to go forever. The moon was full and so bright it almost cast a shadow. Its silver light painted the sea with delicate strokes so it almost seemed to be glowing. Ros had never seen anything like it. Perfectly flat, it stretched into blackness as far as the eye could see. Yet its surface danced as though it was in constant motion. He could hear a thundering from the base of the cliff, where surges of water pounded restlessly against the earth. 'Waves' they were called, he remembered. The combined smell of salt and fish was very strong.

'Weird,' he said.

'Oh, that it is,' Adi agreed.

Bronhill was buzzing up and down on Manton's shoulder, pointing excitedly.

'Is this your first time seeing the ocean?' Manton asked his young charges.

Ros nodded dumbly. It was hard to credit that so much water could exist in the world. 'It looks cold.'

'It could be, this time of year. I advise against going for a swim.'

'How are we going to get across, then?' asked Adi.

Ros cast a sharp look in her direction. They might be trusting Manton in their quest to rescue Varis, but he didn't want any unnecessary talk about Escher and his ultimate aim. One step at a time. 'Why would we want to?'

'To rescue Varis, of course.'

'But we still don't know where he is.'

'What are you talking about? It's right there in front of us.'

'What are *you* talking about, Adi? All I can see is the ocean.'

'There's an island — right there.' She pointed. 'You really can't see it?'

He turned to look at her. She was pointing at nothing, but he knew she wasn't lying. She had been a ghost; she had seen the Weird with her naked eyes; she could see things ordinary people could not.

The way Bronhill was gesticulating suggested that she could see the island too.

'It's hidden,' he said, beginning to understand. 'Charmed in a way I don't understand. That's why I haven't been able to track Varis any further than here.'

'Where is it?' asked Manton, searching the horizon with a hand over his eyes. 'Far away or nearby?'

'Not far,' said Adi. The direction she indicated was to their right by a few degrees. 'We could easily walk there if it wasn't for the water. There's a building of some kind on it. It looks like a ruined fort, but there's light inside. I can see it, just faintly.'

'Firelight?' asked Manton.

'No. It's green.'

They fell silent, considering their strange situation. The only sound came from the ocean. Assuming the island was real, they needed to find a way onto it, and soon. It was only a matter of time before Quirk discovered that the man he had kidnapped wasn't Roslin of Geheb.

'I guess,' said Ros, 'we need to go back to Samimi and rent a boat from Tally Wiskins.'

'You don't need a boat,' said a voice out of the darkness. 'You just need your wits.'

They spun to face the source of the voice. Ros summoned a flame using the Change and cast a cool yellow light out into the darkness.

'Show yourself!' Manton barked. A knife appeared in his hand as though from nowhere.

A strange figure skipped into the light. Human-shaped but not human, child-sized but not a child, the creature possessed narrow features and slender limbs. His eyes were keen and glittered strangely. The clothes he wore were indistinct in the light, but seemed to be made of moss. When he spoke again, his voice was reedy and sharp-toned.

'Douse the flame, Roslin of Geheb, lest you draw more attention to yourself than you already have.'

Ros reduced it to a flicker, unwilling to plunge them into complete darkness. 'You know who I am?'

'Of course. I've been following you from Samimi. My name is Pukje.' He pronounced it *pook-yay*.

'Who are you and what do you want?' Manton asked.

'I want to help you. Am I right in understanding that your friend has been taken prisoner?'

Ros was reluctant to reveal too much until they knew who or what Pukje was, but if the creature could indeed help he was reluctant to send him away. 'A man called Quirk brought him here. We're trying to work out what to do next.'

'The short answer to that question is: nothing.'

'We're not leaving him behind,' said Adi furiously.

'That's not what I mean, girl.' Pukje regarded her curiously. 'Your eyes are keen, like mine. They've stared into the Void, and you use them now to see what others can't. But seeing is not enough. You must understand what you see, and you must reason. Now is not the right time to act.'

'Why not?'

'Are you asking for my advice?'

A warning prickle danced across Ros's skin. He had learnt not to make deals lightly with unknown creatures. 'We're not saying that. We're just asking you a question.'

Pukje turned, his expression more amused than annoyed. 'Wise boy. If you trust your friend here, ask him instead. Ask him about tides.'

Manton looked up sharply. 'Tides? You mean ...? Yes, of course.' He turned to Ros and Adi. 'The sea comes in and out in line with the phases of the moon. It's high tide at the moment, but it won't stay high all night. Soon the sea will retreat, and getting to the island will become a lot easier. We might even be able to walk there under cover of darkness.'

Adi looked sceptical. 'The sea retreats?'

Manton smiled. 'I know that's hard to imagine, but believe me. You'll see for yourself before long.'

'So all we have to do is climb down the cliff, wait for the water to go away and creep across,' Adi said.

'That might be how Quirk himself got there.'

'With his mule?' asked Ros, already thinking that the climbing-down-the-cliff part might be easier imagined than done, especially in the dark.

'There must be a path somewhere. I suggest we search for it while we wait for the tide to turn. We'll have time.'

'Or we could just ask.' Adi turned to put the question to Pukje.

But where the strange creature had stood there was now empty ground.

Ros briefly called his flame higher and held it above his head. There was no sign of Pukje anywhere on the scrubby, flat cliff top.

Silence fell, full of an uncomfortable mix of nervousness and resolve. They knew what they had to do, but very little else. Who or what was Pukje, and what did he want? What lay ahead of them on the island that Ros couldn't even see? How would they defeat Quirk and free Varis before the tide turned again and they were stuck there?

Worse: what if the whole thing were a trap?

'Someone should wait here with Leda and Know-it-All,' Ros said, a lingering suspicion in his mind. 'I think it should be you, Manton.'

The man's broad forehead was furrowed in the light of the moon. 'I can't in good conscience let you go alone.'

'Well, I'm not staying behind,' said Adi, throwing two water bottles into a light pack and slipping it over her shoulder. 'What if Pukje comes back — or worse?'

'But —'

'Look, Varis is our friend so this is our fight,' Ros said. 'We're grateful for your help, Manton, but I think it's best if you don't come any further.'

A war of indecision waged across Manton's face. 'Who says I won't leave and take your mounts with me?'

'Is that what you're going to do?'

Bronhill looked from Adi to Ros to Manton, and shook her head.

'No,' Manton said, sagging. 'I'm not leaving. I'll wait here until you get back, then we'll return to Samimi together.'

'With Varis,' Adi said.

'Yes. I promise.'

Ros watched him carefully. Manton's words said one thing but his demeanour said another. Ros could tell he meant his promise but there was something else going on that he hadn't told them. Manton had never explained why he had helped them in the first place. He owed them nothing. And why was it such a big deal to wait with the animals without them?

'All right,' Ros said, because there was nothing else he could say. An interrogation now would seem ungrateful. 'Knowing you're here with Know-it-All will make me feel better.'

Manton waved away Ros's words with something like irritation and moved the animals back from the cliff edge towards a stand of scrub where they wouldn't be seen from the island. Adi was already edging carefully along the top of the cliff, looking for the way down. Ros stared at the moonlit ocean and pondered how easy it would be to open the leather pouch at his side, remove the quartz prison, and throw it as hard as he could into the water. He really wished it could be so simple.

His legs and back were aching from riding all day. Pukje's sudden appearance had shocked him briefly into alertness, but now his thoughts were foggy and tired. The way ahead was stranger than it had ever been — his destination was literally invisible — but there was no alternative to moving forward.

Gathering his resolve around him like a cloak, he set off after Adi, rescuing Varis foremost on his mind.

3

Ruins by Moonlight

Getting down the cliff proved to be easier than Ros
had feared. Once Adi found the path, it was just a
matter of following it — very carefully, though, because
it was steep and switched backwards and forwards
many times on the way down. Even by moonlight, the
way was difficult to see, and Ros didn't dare light a
flame now. An observer on the island might have
accepted the earlier light as a coincidence — a farmer
looking for a lost animal, perhaps — but someone
descending the cliff was sure to be heading to only one
place.

The bottom of the cliff was a tangle of jagged rocks
and pools of white sand, damp from the ocean's touch.
The surf's incessant pound made him feel as though he
had been caught up in the world's breathing. If he fell
into the water, would he be swept out to sea and sucked
into some enormous lung? The constant motion of the
water was such a contrast to the stillness of the desert,
where only the occasional rain and dust storms ever
wrought any major change. Ros was intrigued to see

that the ocean was indeed retreating, just as Manton and Pukje had said it would. It was like watching the world unpeel its skin and expose the bone beneath.

He stepped lightly onto the wet sand. It gave slightly, accepting his weight with none of the muddiness he had imagined. A brisk wind skirted the base of the cliff, carrying a biting chill with it.

'I still can't see anything,' he told Adi, who had hopped over a rock pool and stood staring up at an apparently empty sky. 'Has the sea gone back far enough yet?'

She looked over her shoulder at him. 'Not unless you're happy to get wet.'

He shivered and looked around for somewhere to shelter. A dark mouth opened in the cliff face not far from where they were standing. He pointed the cave out to Adi, and she agreed that it would be a good place to take cover from the wind while they waited. Although it turned out to be smaller and less comfortable than he had imagined, with only a thick mat of rotting seaweed providing protection from damp rock, at least they weren't going to freeze.

They sat facing each other, their legs braced against the opposite wall and their heads bowed so they didn't bang on the roof above. Time moved slowly, and Ros nodded off on a couple of occasions, to be woken by particularly loud waves. Periodically Adi leaned out to check the water's progress, but always she shook her head. It began to seem that they had been there all night.

'You never told me where you heard that lullaby,' Adi said.

He came out of another semi-sleep with a jolt and forced himself to think. He'd thought that issue long forgotten. 'One of the Clanswomen,' he said. 'Inta, I think. She was singing it.'

'Really? I thought my mother made it up.'

'Maybe you were singing it, then, without knowing it. It got into my head and stuck there. Does it really matter how I know it?'

They sat in silence for a long moment until she said, 'I used to dream about what it was like being a ... you know ... a ghost. I couldn't remember anything that happened in the dreams, but they made me feel strange and unhappy all the same. Then the dreams stopped and I thought they'd never bother me again. But just lately, at weird times, I find myself thinking of things I don't actually remember doing. It's like the dreams have become memories now, and I can think about them. Like I was so afraid of them before that I couldn't let them be part of me, but now I can.'

'That's good, isn't it?' Ros ventured, avoiding her eyes.

'I guess. It's just annoying sometimes because I can never tell what will bring a memory back. You singing that lullaby, for instance. It didn't make me think of my mother, like it should have. Instead I got a flash of a dust storm shouting at me. It reminded me of the dust devil we saw when the Bee Witch died. That was the first one I ever saw. Wasn't it?'

Ros felt torn. He didn't want Adi to know that he had been rummaging through her memories, but at the same time he didn't want to lie to her. 'Dust devils attacked me after the sand bandits stole Know-it-All. That was before Yury found me. You were there too, as a ghost, so you saw the dust devils then.'

'But how does it connect to the lullaby?'

Ros recalled that memory vividly: of Adi complaining to her mother about the way her father was treating her; unwilling to be soothed, not even by that tune from her childhood.

'Beats me,' he said, feigning ignorance. 'If you don't know what's going on inside your own head, how would I?'

'Thanks, Ros.' She poked out her tongue. 'You're a big help.'

He hid his relief as they went back to waiting in silence for the tide to go out.

The moon was far to the west by the time Adi declared it safe to set out. Ros clambered awkwardly from the cave, legs stiff and sore from being confined for so long. The deepening cold didn't help. He tried to keep the chattering of his teeth to a minimum, but even so he feared that Quirk would hear them long before they arrived.

Adi led him in a straight line away from the base of the cliff and set a brisk pace across the soft sand, deviating only to avoid puddles of water in their path. Ros looked behind him and up, but could see no sign of Manton far above. Stars stared coldly back at him, uncaring about his latest adventure. He had heard of people who studied the constellations in order to divine the future and the past. All he saw were twinkling dots on the edge of infinity, unconnected to anything he knew or understood.

A spike of the Change went through him at the very moment his foot struck something half-buried in the sand. With a muffled cry, he tripped forward onto his face.

Adi came back to help him up. He brushed himself down, spitting sodden sand from his mouth. He had landed in a puddle. Now he was colder than ever, and feeling like a fool with it.

'Teach you to walk with your head up in the stars,' she said, not unsympathetically. 'What did you trip over?'

They examined it together: a square slab of stone carved with symbols Ros couldn't read. It buzzed under his hands, so deeply connected was it to the Change. That was what had given him the shock as he tripped. But what was something like that doing buried in a spot usually covered by the sea?

'There's another one. Look.' Adi hurried to where the top of another slab protruded several metres away. 'Could they be a ruin of some kind?'

Ros had his back to the ocean. Only when he turned to say that he had no idea did he see what had until then been invisible to him.

An imposing, steep-sided island jutted out of the gleaming sand directly ahead. Its summit loomed high above them, shaped by unnatural forces into a sharp-tipped spire. He couldn't tell where stone gave way to brick, but it seemed to him that much of the island was artificial. Several squat buildings crowded the base of the spire — or was it one structure with many angles and overlapping faces? In the darkness he couldn't make it out properly.

'You're gawping,' said Adi, coming to stand next to him. 'Does that mean you can see it now?'

He nodded. His eyes tracked past her, to the slabs that lay mostly buried in the waterlogged sand. They seemed to curve in a line between the island and the cliff. This clearly was the charm protecting Quirk's home from sight. By crossing the line, he'd become immune to its effect.

A cold green light shone through a circular window in the spire, just as Adi had described. Ros gleaned little by that light apart from a hint of scaffolding and gleaming metal. Perhaps, he thought, that was where Quirk kept all those old artefacts he collected.

'Can you tell if Varis is in there?' Adi asked.

He tried the hunting charm he had used before. It was difficult to concentrate but he didn't really need to. Varis was so close Ros could practically see him with his real eyes. Quirk was there too, otherwise Ros might have tried to send the Clansman a message. It wasn't worth taking the risk of drawing attention to their presence. They would be there soon enough.

'There's some kind of pipe sticking out the right side,' Adi said, pointing. 'I've been heading that way, thinking it might be a way in.'

'Good idea,' said Ros. 'Lead on.'

She moved unhesitatingly towards a particular section of the island's sheer side. Ros could barely tell it from the rest. His eyes were only slowly adjusting to the new vista before them. The further they went, the more untrustworthy the ground became. If he lingered longer than a second in any one spot, the hungry sand sucked his feet under the surface. Sometimes there was no sand at all underfoot and he dropped with a gasp into a water-filled pothole. Rocks and larger slabs formed a jagged perimeter around the island, waiting for an opportunity to stub toes or crack knees. By the time they squelched up to the base of the island, Ros was bruised and cross and keen for the night to be over.

The pipe Adi had led them to was barely tall enough for them to crouch in. Its sides were slick with slime. Noxious water dripped from the ceiling. From the tunnel's far end came a muffled sound, as of a cloth-wrapped hammer tapping an empty drum. The stench was unbelievable.

'What do you think?' whispered Adi.

'I think we'd better decide soon, before the tide comes back in.'

She gripped her forearms tightly and hopped from one foot to the other. 'All right. Unless you've got any better ideas, this is the way we go.'

'After you.'

'Yeah, I saw that coming,' she said, clambering up into the pipe's gaping maw.

What followed was almost as bad as crawling through crabbler-infested tunnels. The smell was so overpowering Ros barely dared draw breath. He was reluctant to touch the walls but had to because the floor was slippery underfoot. Numerous insects and animals lived in the tunnel, and they were uniformly startled to find humans in their midst. They bit, fled or squirmed according to their natures. But for Adi's determination to keep going, Ros might have turned back and looked for another way in.

The thudding noise grew louder as they ascended into the guts of the island. At first the pipe proceeded in a perfectly straight line, angling steadily upwards for twenty metres, and then it began to rise more steeply. Occasional clots of detritus blocked their path, which they needed to pull free by hand before continuing. Each time Ros was tortured by the fear that the obstacle could not be passed and they would be trapped between it and the rising tide. What if the pipe filled right up and they were drowned? That felt entirely too possible in the slimy, horrid dark.

After an age, he felt Adi slowing ahead. He stopped just an instant after she did, so they were pressed close together in the pipe, both squatting and breathing heavily.

'What is it?'

'Light,' she said over the incessant thumping. 'I can see again.'

He held out his hand and realised that he could too. Barely visible before him was the outline of his fingers. Looking further ahead, he made out the angle and joins of a T-junction. The light — the same green-hued glow that he had seen from below — was issuing from the right-hand path.

'Which way?' she asked.

He searched for Varis and found him immediately. He was still some distance above them and slightly to their left. Quirk was up there too, but to their right.

'Away from the light,' he said.

'Figures.' She grunted and went to move off.

He took her by the shoulder. 'Want me to go first for a while?'

She shuddered. 'Yes, please.'

They awkwardly exchanged places, and Ros led the way to the intersection, then down the left-hand path. The light followed them for a while, revealing that the slime did in fact look as bad as it felt, then it faded again. The sound faded with it, becoming a barely heard beat continuing in the distance. The pipe meandered about before turning into a vertical shaft with a rusty ladder bolted to the side. Ros tested its weight and decided that it would hold him.

'That's the direction we need to go,' he told Adi when she expressed reservations about the ladder holding both of them. 'Do you want to wait here while I go on?'

She shook her head. 'Oh, no. We'll take our chances. It can't be much longer.'

Wishful thinking, Ros thought, but he said nothing.

The slime ran out halfway up the shaft. From there on, not only was it easier to grip the rungs, but the air was less foul. Ros's spirits began to lift. He would find it easier coming back that way with Varis knowing there was an end to it.

The dull thudding — which he reasoned must have been a pump of some kind — was by now completely inaudible. At the top of the ladder, they climbed cautiously up into what might once have been some kind of engine room, but was now full of inert machines that had turned to rust centuries ago. A new sound reached their ears. It was the wind, whistling and moaning with a dozen voices at once, as though a ghostly choir was singing somewhere nearby. The hairs on the back of Ros's neck stood up. Inhuman and dissonant, the sound put his every sense on edge.

They stopped to take a sip of water and decide what to do next. By the light of a very tiny Change flame, they discovered that the engine room was large, with no fewer than three doors leading elsewhere.

'How far now?' Adi asked.

'Closer.'

They had halved the vertical distance to Varis. If they could find a flight of stairs, they could cover the rest in minutes.

Adi used some of her water to wash her hands of drying slime. Ros did the same, and used the corner of his sleeve to clean both their faces. That small effort went a long way to making him feel better, even though it would be days before the stink was out of his nostrils.

When they were rested, they listened at each door to see if they could hear anything. The wind noise was equally strong behind each of them, so they cast lots to pick one at random. The door that drew the longest thread was rusted firmly shut. They tried the second one instead. Its hinges squeaked loudly on opening barely a millimetre. In desperation, they turned to the third and last.

It opened smoothly and without complaint, admitting a chilly gust of wind that took Ros's breath away. He inched forward, seeing by moon and starlight, onto a ledge protruding from the side of the buildings he had glimpsed from the sand far below. There seemed to be three merged into one: two bulbous and smooth, like the walls of a fort, that occupied each end of the oval-shaped island east and west, and the third connecting them, older and more angular. Ros looked up and could see no end to the dark stone wall, down and glimpsed the sparkle of waves. The ledge was barely a metre across, with no handrail or wall.

Adi came up behind him and took stock as well. The moon hung low over the western horizon. It felt as though they had been climbing through the guts of the island for an eternity, but only an hour or so had passed.

Ros went first, holding Adi's hand tightly in case either of them slipped. Barely had they gone three steps when the night was split by a shriek so hate-filled and horrible that his heart almost stopped mid-beat. It came from above, a single angry screech that rose up at the end and echoed wildly around them. Fearing they had been discovered, Ros put his head down and ran.

The ledge led east around the building's smooth waist and then upwards, in a flight of metal stairs. Ros took them two at a time, with Adi close behind. At the top of the stairs was another door — locked, so they could only follow the ledge further around the outside. The wall was as decayed in places as an old tooth. Holes gaped at them. The moment Ros found one large enough to squeeze through, he ducked inside, out of sight, and dragged Adi after him.

The echoes of the shriek were still ringing around them. They clutched each other, afraid that the thing responsible for that noise would reach into their hiding place and snatch them out to a terrible fate.

For all their fear, nothing happened. The echoes faded; no monstrous figure clutched at them through the hole. The moaning of the wind returned, mournful and cold.

A faraway voice reached their ears: 'Master, no — it was a mistake, I swear — all is not lost —'

Then that too was silenced, and all Ros could hear was Adi panting in his ear.

'Was that Quirk?' he whispered, slowly easing his grip on her. It both had and hadn't sounded like him.

'I think so,' she whispered back. 'Who was he talking to? Why did he sound so weird?'

He shook his head, not entirely sure he wanted to know. He took some comfort from the fact that the voices had come from far away.

'Let's find out where we are,' he said.

A tiny flame revealed that they had entered a ruined section of the fort, where the walls, floors and ceiling had fallen away in many places. They moved carefully around black rents and stepped lightly over piles of rubble. The stink of decay was thick in their nostrils. Bricks and mortar crumbled like dirt underfoot.

The green glow had returned, and this time the path to Varis led directly towards it.

Like rats in a wall, they inched deeper into the warren. The fort was clearly ancient and hadn't been evenly maintained. Evidence of age and decay decreased the closer they came to its heart — the ages-old building capped at either end by smooth, impregnable walls. Ros could only guess where the spire stood in relation to the rest. It had seemed to jut out of one end of the island, but until he stumbled across its base or went outside again, he couldn't be sure.

The atmosphere became still and airless, as though living things were discouraged. The temperature rose by several degrees until even the cold became a memory.

Varis was in the island's heart. Quirk was higher up, in some elevated area they hadn't seen yet. Ros hoped he would stay well away.

They took the last few metres very carefully. The light was bright enough to read by now, and the sound of the wind had faded behind them. In the near silence, Ros feared that a single creaking board might ruin everything. They hadn't come so far to fail from a stupid mishap. Who knew who else could be lurking ahead?

Creeping around a corner, they found themselves peering into a cavernous space from a position midway along its length, near the top. It seemed huge enough to house all the buildings of Mount Geheb a dozen times over, and then some. The ceiling was arched and shadowy high above them. Rows of slender columns marched in parallel lines into the distance. Where had once been windows were now bricked over, or turned into passageways to more modern extensions.

That was remarkable enough, but there was more. The heart of the island was crisscrossed with metal girders and stanchions, as though a giant spider had taken up residence and built itself a home in its image. Floors and walkways hung from intersections between the metal strands, connected by ladders and narrow bridges. Knots of metal and glass gleamed in the eerie light, their purpose unknown. A thick green-glowing cable wound from one end of the vast space to the other, looping and curling around the web's intricate beams. Fleeting gleams of light ran along it, casting strange shadows.

Ros's searching gaze locked onto a bell-shaped cage not far from where he and Adi peered out in wonder. A cage containing an unconscious man slumped on his side.

'That's Varis!'

Adi's excited whisper sent echoes dancing. Luckily, apart from Varis, the enormous space was completely empty.

'I think I see a way to get to him,' Ros said.

The opening they were looking through led to a crawlspace that hugged the base of the ceiling's curving arches. They could make their way along it to one of the web's highest anchor-points and climb from there to one of the metal walkways. After that, it was just a matter of reaching the cage, waking Varis, and retracing their steps.

They took a moment to drink from their canteens and then moved out. Adi went first and Ros followed, trying not to think about the drop just centimetres away. The crawlspace was thick with dust and ancient bird droppings.

Adi was in a hurry and set a fast pace. Within a minute, they were at the nearest junction and gathering their courage to swing out to the girder. The metal was solidly bolted and easily strong enough to take their weight; it was even crosshatched with supports, perfect for laddering their way down. It was just the thought of swinging out over that empty air that made them hesitate.

Just as Adi reached out to grasp the girder, a door boomed open far below and someone stepped out into the web, making it rattle.

Adi fell back into the shadows and Ros held his breath. It was Quirk, moving hurriedly from junction to junction in the direction of Varis's cage. The big man looked exactly as Ros had last seen him — clad in travelling clothes and with wild grey hair sticking out in all directions. His expression was furious.

Ros was angry too, with himself for not sensing the man's approach. If Quirk had come a minute later, it would have been a disaster. But a tentative probe with the Change revealed that Quirk had been rendered invisible somehow, just like the island itself. When Quirk reached Varis, it soon became clear how, and why.

Varis didn't react to the rattling and booming of metal around him as Quirk opened the cage with a key. Quirk fussed over the Clansman in a way that seemed nonsensical at first. He cut a lock of dark hair and two slivers of fingernail with a slender knife. Using the blade, he pricked the ball of Varis's thumb and collected a small amount of blood into a glass vial. Into another vial went several drops of Varis's saliva.

Adi looked at Ros with questioning eyes, but he had

no answers. Not until Quirk had completed the strange ritual did he start to understand.

Pulling up his sleeve, Quirk unwound a long, metallic coil from his arm and wrapped it around Varis's forearm. As he did, a strange thing happened. Quirk became visible again through the Change and Varis vanished. The coil, then, was the charm that had hidden Quirk from Ros's view. But when Quirk left the cage and locked the door behind him, something of Varis went with him — an echo of the Clansman that clung to his captor as he hurried through the metal web for the nearest door. Even as Quirk vanished from view, Ros sensed Varis going with him, even though the Clansman remained in the cage right before them.

Comprehension dawned.

'It's a trap,' he whispered to Adi. 'The fingernails, the hair, the blood — Quirk is going to use them to create a lure, a fake Varis, while the real Varis stays hidden. He knows we're coming to the rescue and hopes to draw us somewhere else instead.'

She nodded with widening eyes. 'We're one step ahead. While he's waiting for us somewhere else, we can get Varis out of that cage and safely off the island. Easy!'

Ros nodded with relief. He could track Quirk now, and that gave them an extra edge they hadn't had before.

Buoyed by the upswing in their fortune, first Adi then Ros eased out onto the scaffolding. Moving slowly and carefully, they climbed into the web. Their every movement set it swaying, no matter how careful they were. But for the moment they were undisturbed. Quirk was busy elsewhere, and the rest of the fort was quiet.

Adi ran the last few metres when they reached the ramp leading to Varis's cage. She tried the door, but it was firmly bolted. Getting in was up to Ros, who had learnt to pick locks with his mind when escaping from the inn in Barker. Shifting tumblers was a small thing compared to confining golems or battling killer bees. It took only a moment's concentration before the lock clunked and the cage door swung open.

Adi was instantly at the Clansman's side, shaking him. 'Varis, wake up!'

Varis groaned and his eyes flickered, but he remained firmly unconscious.

Adi turned to Ros with worry in her eyes. 'You have to do something. We can't carry him.'

Ros knelt next to her. Varis looked completely unharmed, so his persistent slumber couldn't be natural. The metallic spiral Quirk had applied remained tightly wrapped around his left forearm. Ros left it there, not wanting to unnecessarily alert anyone to the fact that their charms were being tampered with. When he tugged at the Clansman's tunic, he found a different charm wrapped around Varis's neck.

'Have you ever seen that before?' he asked Adi.

'No.'

'Then that's the charm.'

Ros reached for it, intending to pull it from the sleeping man's throat. The moment his fingers touched the metal, he slumped over onto his side, unconscious.

He woke to Adi's hands violently shaking him. 'Come on, Ros. Snap out of it!'

He blinked and sat up. 'What? Oh, sorry.'

Blearily he studied the charm again. Touching it had clearly drawn him under its influence as well. This time he kept the collar of Varis's shirt carefully between the charm and his fingers, and managed to unwind it and toss it to one side. When it hit the floor of the cage, it curled up into a ball like a dead spider and emitted a puff of acrid smoke.

Instantly, Varis's eyelids fluttered. He looked blankly at Ros and Adi, then sat up with a jerk. 'The stables — someone —'

'Don't worry about that,' said Adi, shushing him. 'We were ambushed and you were kidnapped, but we've found you now. All we have to do is escape. Can you walk?'

The Clansman rose unsteadily to his feet and looked around, puzzled. 'Where am I?'

They quickly brought him up to date on the island and the charm Quirk had used to hide him. 'If we're quick,' Adi said, 'we'll be gone before he suspects a thing.'

'I'm sorry you had to go to so much trouble because of my mistake.' Varis smiled with a fondness he rarely expressed. 'Adi, your father would be very proud.'

She fairly glowed. 'It wasn't your mistake — it was Quirk's — and I know you would have done the same for us.'

'That's my duty. We're family.'

Ros was distracted by a tickling at the back of his mind. The illusion of Varis was stationary somewhere above them, but Quirk was on the move again.

'Let's go,' he said. 'We don't want to be caught like this.'

'Okay.' Varis put himself protectively in the lead as they left the cage. 'Which way did you come?'

Adi showed him the route they had followed down the web. It seemed much longer than it had when they came up.

'Why go up when we'll just have to go back down again?' Varis said. 'There are other ways out. That door down there, for instance. It must go somewhere.'

'I don't know,' said Ros, uncertainty making his gut roil. It wasn't the same exit Quirk had used, but that didn't mean it was safe. 'What if we get lost?'

'What if Quirk comes back before we get up on that ledge?' Varis's jaw was set. 'We'll be trapped.'

'All right ... I guess.'

They made their way through the creaking web, trying to keep noise to a minimum. The glowing green cable swayed, casting strange shadows across the walls. Sometimes they looked like people moving at the corner of Ros's eyes, making him even more jumpy than he already was. Quirk was still some distance away, but they knew he could move quickly when he had to.

The exit Varis had indicated wasn't so much a door as a hole in the stone wall leading to another section of the sprawling structure. There were no locks to negotiate, no bolts or bars. Ros's heart began to race as they drew nearer. Could escape be as easy as simply running out the front door?

He neither saw nor heard a thing as they passed over the threshold. However, a sudden flare in the Change told him that life did indeed intend to make things difficult for them again.

'Wait.' He took Adi's arm. 'Something happened.'

'What do you mean?'

Ros concentrated. Quirk had stopped dead. There was no alarm, no shouts from elsewhere in the fort, but Ros was certain their passage had been noticed. As he watched, Quirk started moving again — faster than before, with determination and purpose, right for them.

'Run!' Ros hissed. 'He knows we're here!'

Varis nodded and took both their hands. They fled the giant chamber and ran along a broad brick corridor that clearly saw a lot of use. There were no holes in the floors to negotiate and the air smelled fresh. At the first intersection, they used their noses to guide them. They had come through foul, dripping tunnels, and it was by those tunnels they would escape. Anywhere clean or wholesome was to be avoided. The sound of their running feet echoed around them, and Ros kept his mental eye on Quirk as best he could, lest his would-be kidnapper came too close on their heels.

'This way!' Adi pulled them through a rotting door, which collapsed to splinters in their wake, and out onto a wide rooftop.

The air was bitingly cold, but the moon was gone and a faint glow on the eastern horizon revealed that dawn wasn't far away. The three of them cut diagonally across the roof to where another door hung invitingly open. Ros thought he recognised the shape of that wing of Quirk's domain; they had passed near there on their way in.

His relief died on finding their way blocked by a massive hole in the floor that stretched right across their path. Two narrow wooden beams were all that spanned the hole, and they looked decidedly unsteady.

Adi wasn't easily deterred. She tested the first beam, and it held. Moving lightly and quickly, she took three steps across it and reached the far side.

'You next, Ros,' said Varis, pushing him forward.

'What about you?'

'I'll come last. I'm heavier.'

Ros couldn't delay. He had to trust both the beam and his balance. Not daring to think, he did as Adi had done and ran across the beam. She clutched at him when he reached safety. The whites of her eyes were bright in the gloom.

Varis was midway between his second and third step when a shriek broke the silence, as loud as the first they had heard but even more frightening, if that were possible. It froze Ros's heart and made the Clansman stumble. His foot slipped on the beam and he lost his balance. Ros saw him struggle to regain it, putting more weight than he should have on the very centre of the beam. It cracked with a noise like a whip, and Ros held onto Adi with all his strength to stop her leaping to Varis's aid. There was no use both of them falling.

But Varis didn't fall. As the beam broke under him, he leapt sideways, awkwardly but effectively, and caught the second beam at chest height. It rained dust and creaked, but held the Clansman's weight. With a grunt, he hauled himself upright and crawled to safety.

He was sweating when he reached them, and his hands were shaking. 'Let's not wait around to find out what's making that noise,' he said.

'Agreed,' said Adi. 'I can hear the pump again too.'

She was right. Ros hadn't noticed the steady thumping coming from ahead of them, but they followed the sound now as though it were a thread leading them through a maze.

'Where's Quirk?' Adi asked him, and he was horrified to realise that he hadn't been checking.

Through the Change, he saw the man closing the distance between them with formidable speed. 'We have to hurry,' he said, and pulled Adi to their right and pushed Varis ahead of him. There wasn't a second to waste.

They wound through ruined halls and along decrepit corridors. His gut told him they were heading in the right direction, and that was confirmed when they came to a door leading to the ledge he and Adi had followed earlier that night. The sky was becoming pink as they ran pell-mell for the engine room. When it came into view, he began to believe they might actually make it.

'Stop!' The cry came from behind them. It was Quirk, puffing but managing with his long strides to keep up with them. 'Stop right there!'

'Keep going,' Ros said to Adi. 'I'll slow him down.'

Ros turned and concentrated. He was exhausted but the Change was all around him and all through him. It rushed into him and buoyed him up. Suddenly he felt light and air-filled, not tired at all.

Quirk had halved the distance between them when the ledge kicked underfoot. Ros steadied himself, and pushed again. A desk-sized chunk of the ledge shattered to gravel two steps ahead of Quirk and rained down into the sea below. Quirk skidded to a halt and recoiled from the drop. Ros encouraged him by knocking away another section of ledge, making certain the gap was too far to jump.

Quirk shook his fist at him. 'You'll be sorry you did that!'

Ros turned his back on him and ran to catch up with Adi and Varis.

The engine room was exactly as they had left it. Rusted hulks filled the high-ceilinged space. A series of slimy footprints marked where Ros and Adi had emerged from the vertical pipe and taken a moment to rest. He had become so accustomed to the stink that it barely registered now, but he saw Varis's face screw up in disgust. Ros didn't care. He just wanted to get back to Know-it-All and ride far away.

'After you this time,' said Adi, indicating the pipe.

But as Ros stepped forward, there was a tearing crash and the door they had tried first but found to be rusted shut burst off its hinges. It fell to the ground with a single dent in its centre, caused by the blow that had smashed it open. A cloud of rust rose up, obscuring the doorway. Ros went to put Adi behind him, but she wasn't going to hide from anything.

Through the door stepped something that was not man, machine or man'kin, but a mixture of all three. It had two arms and two legs and a forward-thrusting, domed head with two glowing eyes. Its limbs were made from metal and wood and leather, tangled up in a strange parody of muscle, skin and bone. Light shone around its wiry joints and sinews. With a metallic clatter it swivelled its head and tracked its green-glowing gaze across the room. One claw-like hand lifted to point at Ros, who stood dwarfed before its unnatural size and reach.

'You,' it said in a voice like steam from a kettle. 'The boy-thing.'

Ros backed away, all strength leached from him. The thing before them was undoubtedly the source of the screaming he and Adi had heard. It was the mastermind behind the plan to kidnap Varis.

Not Varis, he reminded himself. Roslin of Geheb. *Him.*

Hissing and clanking, the creature took a step forward.

'Keep away!' shouted Varis, putting himself in its path.

It made a noise like a snarl and swept Varis aside. Its limbs were spindly, but they had the strength of a catapult. 'You have caused me enough inconvenience already, man-thing.'

Varis went down hard. Adi screamed.

Ros wanted to scream too, but the breath was caught in his throat. As the thing approached, he retreated, putting one of the hulks between it and him.

Its rattling steps pursued him. 'You have something I wish to possess,' the thing wheezed. 'You will give it to me.'

'We're not giving you anything,' Adi yelled at it. 'Leave us alone!'

Ros dodged as the thing caught sight of him and juddered forward. 'Quit your clamour, girl-thing. You are no concern of mine.'

'Oh no?' Adi appeared from behind one of the hulks holding a broken metal rod. She lashed out with it and struck the machine-creature behind its left knee.

With a roar, it staggered backwards. Top-heavy and cumbersome, it flailed for balance and fell.

'Quickly, Ros!' She was at his side, tugging him after her. 'It's too big to fit down the pipe. Help me with Varis! We can still do this!'

The sound of the creature thrashing around filled the engine room. Varis was stirring when they reached him, and bleeding from a cut above the eye. Ros and Adi managed to get him to his feet and together the three of them staggered to the pipe.

'You first, Adi,' the Clansman insisted. 'Then Ros.'

Adi was barely halfway into the pipe when hands made of flesh and blood snatched at Ros from behind and pulled him from his friends. 'No!' he cried, twisting to catch a glimpse of Quirk's determined visage. The man's grip was too tight to escape from. 'Let me go!'

Adi froze, terrified, as Quirk's mechanical master hove into view, hissing and creaking like overworked bellows.

'Don't stop!' Varis ordered her, tugging something from his arm and giving it to her. 'You'll be safe if you keep going!' Then he picked up the metal pipe she had dropped and drew himself up to his full height.

But Quirk's master was unstoppable. It blocked two powerful blows from the Clansman, then caught the pipe in one hand and wrenched it away from him. Varis ducked one knock-out punch, then another. The creature's whiplash strength was more powerful than a man's, but it was about as agile as a tractor. If Varis hadn't been recently charmed and almost knocked out, he could have led the thing a dance for hours.

Ros was poised to strike with the Change when a miscalculation on Varis's part saw him clipped across the temple. He fell bonelessly to the ground, and this time he didn't get up.

In fury, Ros reached deep into himself and lashed out at Quirk's inhuman master. *Burn*, he told the thing's wooden skeleton. *Melt*, he ordered its wiry sinews. *Shatter*, he instructed its crystal eyes. *Die*.

Nothing happened. Utterly untouched, the creature stepped over Varis's body and walked towards Ros, its fingers outstretched like the hands of a skeleton.

Ros tried again, so hard his head rang with the effort. A throbbing hum rose up in his temples, and he felt a line of blood pour from his nose over his lips. Still the thing approached.

The third time Ros tried almost turned him inside out. Nothing. Through eyes hazed over with effort, he saw a charm swinging from the creature's spindly neck, another intricate, brassy creation like the one Quirk had placed on Varis.

It's protected, he belatedly realised. *The Change can't touch it.*

With greedy fingers it reached for him and he was too weak to pull away.

'Yes,' it grated. 'At last it is mine.'

Its hands went not to Ros's throat, but to the leather pouch at his side.

'No,' Ros moaned, feeling consciousness slipping from him and trying his best to fight it. He had wasted his energy and now he was helpless. 'You can't have that!'

'It's all I want, boy-thing. It's all I've ever wanted.'

In desperation, Ros looked for Adi in the entrance to the pipe. Just her eyes and the top of her head were visible. She was weeping with impotent rage.

Help, he mouthed. *Get help!*

There was nothing Adi could do on her own. He didn't blame her when she ducked out of sight and retreated into the island's depths. The two of them had failed to save Varis; they had, in fact, made things much worse. She needed to survive and find Manton, their one and only remaining hope. Perhaps the two of them could work out what to do next.

Quirk chuckled nastily. Spindly fingers plucked at the Golem of Omus's crystal prison. Ros felt no lightness as his terrible burden was taken from him, only darkness, sweeping him away.

4

The Scarecrow's Plan

Ros was searching, first for Escher and then for Adi. Neither, however, could be found. He ran across beaches and dunes, through scrub and farmland, calling their names in a loud voice, but they never answered. Where had they gone? Why had they left him? He had become so used to them whispering into his ear. How could he survive without them?

Then he remembered that Adi was no longer a ghost and could talk to him like an ordinary person. But that only made him more anxious. If she was back in her body and no longer invisible, how had she become lost? How had he let her get away?

By stages he understood that he was dreaming. He struggled awake with Adi's absence in the forefront of his thoughts. His head still reeled, but the Change was returning to him. He reached out for it, hunting for Adi as he had hunted Varis and Quirk. She couldn't have gone far. If he could touch her mind, he would be able to stop worrying about her.

He searched and found nothing, not on or in the

island, nor on the beach or the cliffs. Manton, Leda and Know-it-All stood out like beacons. Their new friend's promise had held. Adi, however, was nowhere to be seen.

Ice-cold water flooded through his veins at the thought that she might be dead.

Then he remembered the thing that Varis had tossed her before she vanished down the pipe to freedom: the charm that had made him invisible. That was why Ros couldn't see her. She was hidden, not gone for good.

'He's doing it again,' said a voice. 'Shall I increase the flow to the restraints?'

A mechanical hiss greeted the announcement. 'Yes, but what wasted energy! The boy-thing is more powerful than I expected.'

'Perhaps we should get rid of him then, Master, along with his friend.'

'I do not consider him to be a danger to us here in the cathedral. Do you, Quirk?'

'Of course not, Master —'

'Then do as you have been instructed. The two of them may yet prove valuable.'

Ros felt as though a heavy blanket had fallen over him. His eyes fluttered. Blurrily he made out a cage bathed in green light, and the grey-haired man circling it, making adjustments with some kind of tool. The mechanical creature stood behind Quirk, as motionless as a man'kin.

Ros's hands were bound tightly behind his back. He was clearly a prisoner in the metal web at the heart of the island, but that didn't worry him as much as the realisation that the Change was leaving him. His ability to search outside the cage collapsed; he could barely feel Varis lying right next to him. It seemed the fuzziness in his head had nothing to do with overextending himself, after all. Quirk and his master were doing it to him deliberately, to stop him exercising any of his special abilities. The fear that he might be trapped forever made him actively struggle against the restraints, physically and through the Change. Blue sparks flashed from the top of the cage.

'Master, he resists!'

'So try harder, Quirk. Increase the flow to the charms again. He is only human. We will prevail over him!'

Ros gritted his teeth, determined to prove the creature wrong, but almost immediately realised the foolishness of doing that. *If I fight*, he thought, *they'll just keep fighting back. Maybe they'll beat me; maybe I'll beat them, at great cost. Either way, better to let them think they've won and keep some strength in reserve for when I need it.*

Feigning exhaustion, he let himself sag, panting, onto the floor of the cage. His eyes stayed open. There was no point maintaining that pretence now.

Quirk continued to fiddle with the cage, even though the showers of sparks had ceased. His dark eyes studied Ros with suspicious fascination from under thickly bushed brows. He had changed out of his travelling clothes into a stained black robe with floppy sleeves. His master hadn't moved throughout the entire confrontation. Ros could see that it was connected to the glowing green cable by a slender thread that disappeared into its complicated-looking midsection. Its eyes glowed a steady green to match.

'What are you?' Ros asked the bizarre creature. 'What do you want with the crystal?'

'Not the crystal, boy-thing.' It came closer, making the web sway underfoot. Its movements were tentative, like an arthritic old man's. 'What it contains.'

'But it doesn't contain anything,' he lied. 'It's just a trinket my father gave me.'

'Do not lie to me. Quirk uncovered the truth of it from your family and from the golem-hunter called Kuller. They witnessed the transformation of the Golem of Omus. They spoke proudly of your achievement.'

Proudly? His family? Ros couldn't believe it. 'You're lying. Quirk didn't speak to anyone. He's just guessing.'

A nasty grin spread across Quirk's face. 'You named the golem "Sherec". I couldn't guess that, could I?'

Ros's face burned. That was true. Quirk knew everything.

'So what?' he said. 'What does it matter what I did?'

'It matters a great deal to me.' The creature reached into its workings and disconnected the glowing umbilical cord. 'I am the Scarecrow,' it said, coming right up to the cage and peering in at him. Suddenly its movements were smooth and sure and startlingly fast. 'You have brought me a very powerful boon, at some inconvenience to yourself. What can I offer you in return?'

Ros's head spun. Whatever it was, the Scarecrow had to be completely insane. First it kidnapped Varis; then it stole Escher's prison from him; now it wanted to give him something to make him feel better?

'Just give me the crystal back,' he said. 'It's dangerous. If the golem ever gets out —'

'Have no fear on that score, boy-thing.' Tiny cogs and gears, as translucent as the wings of flies, were visible through gaps in the Scarecrow's metal-plated skull, turning with a constant whirr and whisper. 'Your old friend will never see the light of day again.'

'He was never my friend,' Ros said, feeling the sting of that betrayal all over again. 'And my name is not "boy-thing". It's Ros.'

The Scarecrow tsked in annoyance, a sound like hot metal cooling. 'Humans all look alike to me. Fleeting, pesky creatures. But I needed you, and I understand your concerns, and I know that I must offer recompense for this thing I have taken. That is the nature of commerce. The people you travel with understand that too.'

Ros thought of Adi, and hoped she was well away from this madhouse. 'Will you let me and Varis go, if that's what I ask for?' he said.

'Of course.'

'What if you're lying?'

'If I meant you ill, you would have died in your sleep.'

Another good point. But Quirk's scowl suggested that it might have been a close call.

'I need to think about it,' Ros said, conflicting impulses making what should have been a simple decision much harder. He could win his freedom — something that had seemed unlikely just minutes earlier — but only by leaving Escher behind; only by failing to fulfil the vow that he had made to himself to drop the

Golem of Omus into the deep ocean, where it would never, ever be found. 'Do I have to decide now?'

'I will give you some time,' said the Scarecrow, pulling back from the cage. 'You will remain encaged, however, while you contemplate.'

Ros hadn't expected otherwise. 'All right. Where will you be?'

'In my laboratory, making preparations. Quirk will attend you.'

The Scarecrow clanked and hissed through the web and exited via the nearest door. Quirk bowed as his master passed, then turned a baleful stare on his captives.

'I saw what you did to Kuller,' he said. 'If you try anything like that on me —'

'I won't,' Ros promised, still ashamed of how he had burnt the golem-hunter, 'if you don't hurt me or Varis. Why is he asleep? Have you charmed him again?'

The Clansman was unmoving apart from the shallow rise and fall of his chest.

'You broke the last sleeping charm we had,' Quirk said. 'They don't grow on trees, you know.'

'Where *do* you get them from?' Ros asked, his curiosity roused. As well as the sleeping charm there was the device hiding Adi from view, the island's camouflage, and the charm that had put everyone in the Coach and Camel to sleep. 'I've never seen anything like these things before.'

A prideful gleam came to Quirk's eye. 'We make them,' he said. 'The Scarecrow and I. My master possesses knowledge you can only dream of.'

'Make them out of what?'

'Relics of the old times.'

Ros remembered what Manton had told him and Adi about the kind of merchandise Quirk scoured the market for. 'How do you turn a piece of old junk into something useful?' he asked.

'Sometimes the junk is irrelevant. Age alone can be enough, for time is the vehicle of change. *The* Change.' Quirk caught himself, as though on the verge of saying too much. 'You don't need to know,' he said, fussing about the cage with the tool he had used to adjust the restraints — a silver rod with a curved end like a crochet hook. 'You just need to accept my master's offer and leave us in peace.'

Ros had time to study Quirk as he went about his business. He could look tall and hale when he needed to, but his back naturally slumped and there were sores beneath his beard. A weariness about him spoke of years of servitude.

'You know, the Scarecrow didn't answer my question,' Ros said. 'It didn't tell me what it was.'

'My master will never talk about that,' said Quirk, casting him a pointed look. 'I advise you to save your breath.'

Quirk pottered about a while longer, and Ros watched him, wanting to ask about his family but lacking the courage to do so. What did he want to hear? That they were perfectly happy, or missing him desperately?

Questions he could live with. Answers were ever the problem.

Varis's head had long ceased bleeding, judging by the dried bloodstain on his face and neck, but still he didn't wake up. Ros made him as comfortable as possible. There was little else he could do for him. While Quirk was busy elsewhere in the web with his chores, he explored the cage and its restraints. He wanted to try to look for Adi again.

The cage was different from the one Varis had been held in. This was a spherical affair, an intricate construction of brass and silver that was attached by several green wires to the main channel threaded through the web. Ros had yet to work out what the green energy was that caused the light, but it was obviously connected to the workings of the cage and the Change-sapping charm that kept him from breaking free.

He touched the bars all around the cage, hesitantly at first then with greater confidence. Direct contact didn't make the charm stronger or weaker. It just tickled slightly. He detected a flow of energy through the metal that felt exactly like the Change. Could that be what the green cable provided — the Change itself?

That was a puzzling thought. The Change was the energy of life. It hadn't occurred to him that it could be tamed and stored in anything that wasn't living. Presumably that was how someone with no natural affinity for the Change, like Quirk, could attain a small degree of mastery over it.

Ros felt a tap on his shoulder and turned around, startled.

The cage was empty apart from him and Varis, who slept on undisturbed.

His ear registered the tap this time, and he snatched with his left hand at something dancing in the corner of his eye. It was a pebble dangling from a hair-thin thread.

The moment his skin touched the thread, a voice spoke directly into his mind.

(Guess who?)

He looked up in surprise, following the thread into the shadows of the ceiling. The voice belonged to the strange little man who had told them to wait for the tides before approaching the island. Ros couldn't see him, but he remembered his name. Pukje had disappeared into the night as though never to return. What was he doing here, and how could he be talking to him this way, as Adi's ghost had?

(Don't make a sound, Ros, or Quirk will become suspicious. I'm here to help you. Nod if you understand.)

He thought quickly. Pukje had led him truly once. There was no reason to mistrust him now. Perhaps Pukje was talking to him this way because it couldn't be overheard.

Ros dropped his head to his chest then raised it again.

(Don't pull too hard on the thread,) came the voice in his mind, (or you'll break it. Let me give you some slack so you can sit. It'll look more natural that way.)

Ros folded his legs underneath him and came down next to Varis.

(The thread allows us to talk without interfering with the restraints,) Pukje said. (You can respond, if you're careful. I know you've learnt how to throw your thoughts. You spoke to Kuller that way, once.)

Ros's hand holding the pebble clenched into a fist. Did *everyone* know what he had done before coming to Samimi?

(What —) Ros stopped when the cage sparked in response, prompting Quirk to look up. He waited a moment, and, when Quirk looked away, tried again, more gently this time. (What's going on here? Why have they taken my crystal?)

(I'll tell you, but first we have to loosen your chains. That cage you're in is like a giant sponge. It'll soak up anything you try to throw at it and discharge it into the ocean. There's one easy way to stop a sponge soaking up water. Do you know what it is, Ros?)

Ros thought for a second. (Make sure it's completely soaked first?)

(That's exactly right. I'm going to show you how to reverse the flow of the Change to make the energy in the ocean fill up the cage's reservoirs. That way it won't be able to take anything from you, but it won't sound an alarm either. It won't be broken; it'll just be working improperly.)

Pukje paused as though waiting for questions. Ros's head was reeling. For the moment, he had none.

(Right. Shuffle over so your shoulder is touching the cage. You'll need to be connected to the circuit before you can interfere with it. Good. Now, send your thoughts into the flow. Feel the direction it's going; let yourself drift with it. Don't be afraid of getting tangled up in it; that's not what the trap is designed to do. It just wants to guide the Change from one place to another. It's an arrow on a wall, telling the Change which way to go. You're going to turn that arrow around and then we'll be on our way.)

Ros did as he was told. It was easy to fall back into old patterns of behaviour. He had missed being guided by a bodiless voice, and Pukje made no claims of friendship or loyalty. He just made sense. And what he told Ros to do worked. He could feel the flow of energy in the cage and bend it to his will. Without a single spark, without rousing Quirk's suspicion in the slightest, Ros felt his full connection to the Change return.

The first thing he did was reach out for Adi, but she was still hidden by the charm Varis had given her.

(Don't do anything rash,) Pukje said. (You're in no position to escape just yet. Even with my help, you're not going to be able to take your friend with you.)

Ros saw the sense in that, although it required all his willpower not to reach out and set Quirk's bushy hair on fire.

(And don't let go of the thread,) Pukje added. (That's the only thing connecting us. Without it, you could talk to me but I couldn't reply.)

(Why not?)

(Unlike you, I have no natural affinity for the Change. But that doesn't mean I'm helpless. You don't have to have the Change to know how it works. Aids such as this thread will do, just like the Scarecrow and his pawn make do with. Needs must when the devil drives, eh?)

That explained why he was talking like a ghost. Adi had no talent for the Change either. (How did you get here, then? It's daylight now. You must've had some way to hide yourself on the beach.)

(A distraction was all I needed. You amply provided that. And who's to say I wasn't here already, when you arrived?)

(If you had been, you would've helped us.)

(Don't be so sure of that. I make a habit of avoiding fights.)

(Even if the Scarecrow had killed us?)

(It wasn't going to. For all its faults, the Scarecrow does possess its own kind of honour.) Pukje's voice was very serious. (Ros, I need to talk to you about something.)

(What?)

(I've helped you twice now, and I want to help you again, but from now on you should know that my help doesn't come for free. In return, you have to promise to do something for me.)

Ros tried to hide his uncertainty. His instinct to avoid committing himself to anyone he didn't know warred with his need to trust the voice whispering into his mind. Pukje *had* helped him. Wasn't that worth something?

(Tell me what you want,) Ros said. (Then maybe I'll promise.)

(It may not sound like much, but I'm not going to fool you. It'll be difficult, and I know you'll be tempted to change your mind more than once. I'll only help you escape the Scarecrow if you take the Golem of Omus with you. That's my sole condition. The crystal must not remain in the Scarecrow's hands. Will you promise that?)

Ros frowned. What did it matter to Pukje what happened to Escher?

(I don't understand.)

(I know, but when you've agreed, I'll do my best to help you understand. That much I promise you in return. I can't pretend to be completely trustworthy, but in this instance I am a creature of my word.)

The choice was a difficult one — between a living machine and an imp-like being of unknown allegiance — and the deals they offered were very different. Ros couldn't agree to both of them. If he left without the golem, could he trust the Scarecrow to dispose of it safely? It had said that Escher would never see the light of day again, but it could easily have been lying. As soon as Ros was gone, it might smash the crystal and let the Golem of Omus loose on another rampage.

Pukje's admissions of his own limitations were the deciding factor in the end. He described himself as untrustworthy, and that somehow made him seem more honest. Ros decided that he would trust Pukje far enough to guarantee Escher's retrieval. Beyond that he would watch his back.

(All right,) Ros said, (but only if you promise that I can take the crystal with me when I leave the island.)

(I had no intention of letting you do otherwise. That's good. In a moment I'm going to ask you to let go of the thread, but first you have to find me. Close your eyes and look up.)

Only with the Change was it possible to comply with such a paradoxical request. Ros did as he was told and sent his point of view up into the shadows of the ceiling, following the thread to its source.

Pukje was squatting on a dusty beam with knobbly knees pressed against his chest and the thread held lightly in narrow, long-fingered hands. Ros struggled to manage two charms at once — that of seeing outside his body and talking with his mind alone — but with concentration he could manage it.

(I see you,) he said.

Pukje didn't look at him because there was nothing of him to be seen. He did, however, blink his right eye, which struck Ros as odd until he asked, (Which eye did I just close?)

(Right,) Ros said, and the little man nodded.

(Excellent. Now, let go of the thread and follow me. Quietly. There's a lot of sensitive equipment where I'm about to take you.)

Ros instructed his distant hands to release the pebble, and watched as Pukje wound the thread around two of his fingers and disappeared it into a fold of his strange clothes. Then he was on his feet and moving lightly and surely through the maze of beams and ledges high above Ros's cage. He never once looked down.

Ros followed closely, wondering what Pukje was going to show him. Was it a way out? But Pukje was going up not down, and soon it became clear that he was taking Ros along ways that no human could follow, not even a child. He squeezed through cracks and crawled along pipes with the ease of a rat, moving surely even in darkness and making no sound at all. Ros could hear as well as see; he supposed he could move things if he wanted to, by combining charms again. He had never thought of doing that before.

Pukje emerged from a crawlspace onto the roof of the island's heart, and scampered on light feet across the eastern rooftop. In the bright daylight, Ros saw the spire looming large over them and guessed that this was where they were heading.

With the agility of a lizard, Pukje scaled the spire's nearest side and slipped into the shadow of its conical roof. From there he moved more slowly, barely disturbing the cobwebs he passed. Ros could see imprints of tiny hands and feet in the dust and knew that Pukje had been this way before.

A shaft of greenish light shone from a chink in the ceiling, and Pukje pressed close against it to peer into the room below.

Ros didn't need such a peephole. He needed only to propel his point of view forward in order to explore the room at will. When he went to do so, however, he found his point of view blocked by an invisible barrier. The room was charmed.

He didn't push. The barrier might be alarmed as well as invisible. Slipping between Pukje and the barrier, he took in the scene as best he could.

The Scarecrow stood as still as a statue directly below, connected via one of the thin green tubes to the main cable. It was watching a small, red-mouthed furnace in which something metallic gleamed. The room was lined with orderly benches weighed down by charms and artefacts. A length of green cable hugged the circular walls, providing light in what was obviously the Scarecrow's laboratory. Strange combinations of individual charms loomed on all sides. One looked like a metallic flower with spiny petals in an open position. Another was a cup of finely blown glass, blackened and sooty around the edges. A third resembled a telescope Ros had once seen a trader show off, only it was much larger, mounted on a sturdy tripod and pointed at a stone wall. Irregular pulses and vibrations came to Ros through the Change as all around the laboratory lights flickered, tiny clockwork mechanisms whirred and multicoloured flames guttered and flared.

A bell rang and the Scarecrow moved. With a pair of iron tongs, it reached into the furnace and removed a glowing, brassy knot. It dipped the complex metal shape into a bath of cooling water and placed it into the blackened glass cup. And then it did a very strange thing indeed. With precise, mechanical steps, it crossed to the far side of the room and plucked an armful of rusty artefacts from a teetering pile near the door. Carrying them to the flower-like basket, it placed them inside, one at a time, and then closed the folding 'petals' over them.

Ros felt a tingle in the Change as the Scarecrow crossed to a bank of switches and pulled the largest one. A whirring noise rose up out of the silence. The green glow flickered. Sparks cracked and popped, and a smell of metallic smoke bloomed.

A loud bang signalled the end of the process. The Scarecrow raised the switch and went to inspect the object it had placed in the glass cup. Holding it aloft in both hands and turning it from side to side, the Scarecrow nodded, satisfied.

Ros watched, fascinated. The object was a charm, but it hadn't been a moment ago. It had just been a lump of metal, as Change-full as a brick. Now it hummed with power.

The Scarecrow clanked to a large tangle of other charms it was constructing on one of the tables. The new charm slotted perfectly into place alongside its neighbours, becoming part of a much larger work in progress. Then the Scarecrow returned to the metal basket, scooped out the artefacts and tossed them into a rubbish chute near the original pile. They clattered to oblivion, their purpose fulfilled.

Ros took it all in and made a kind of sense out of it. Quirk had told him that the Scarecrow made charms by sucking the Change out of old artefacts. That must have been what he had just witnessed. But why did Pukje want him to see what the Scarecrow was up to? How did it relate to him and his problems?

Pukje reached past him to point down into the workshop at something in particular, and Ros felt the charms he was using tremble on the point of dissolution.

His crystal rested on a silver plate on a bench all to itself. That was what Pukje wanted him to see. There was the Golem of Omus, without which he had promised not to leave — in the Scarecrow's laboratory on the other side of the island, separated from him by an invisible barrier that his mind could not break.

'I see it,' Ros whispered with his mind, not able to talk like a ghost via the charmed thread any more. 'How am I going to get it out of there?'

Pukje backed away from the peephole and climbed up to the top of the spire's roofline. There was a hatch. Outside, the air was clear and fresh, and the sky seemed endlessly blue. The contrast to the green gloom of the Scarecrow's lair could not have been greater.

Pukje squatted on the roof's highest point and said aloud, 'I don't know, Ros. We'll find a way. What's important right now is that you know what the Scarecrow is doing. I overheard Quirk talking to you earlier. You saw how the Scarecrow takes the Change out of old artefacts and puts it into new ones. What you may not know is that the Change doesn't just go into charms. It goes into the Scarecrow's own body too. That's how it lives. It's like a Change vampire.'

Ros didn't know what a vampire was, but it sounded pretty gruesome. 'It eats the Change?'

'Only what it can drain through its machine. You saw that working a moment ago. Artefacts go in one end; the Change comes out the other, like juice when you squeeze an orange. The Scarecrow can use it any way it wants, once the Change is in that form.

'You also saw the new machine it's building — a collector just like the other, only much bigger and capable of sucking out much larger amounts of the Change. The Scarecrow has been working on this machine for months.'

'How do you know all this?'

'I keep my eyes open. I see what's important.'

'Why is this important? The Scarecrow isn't hurting anyone. It's just buying old stuff and living off it. If it was stealing from or hurting people —'

'The world doesn't revolve around people, Ros. There are other things in it too, like me. Think carefully before you dismiss the Scarecrow's actions as harmless. What would happen if it put your friend's pet man'kin into the collector? It would drain her of everything that makes her alive and pump it into its own organs.'

Ros shuddered at the thought. 'I guess it could.'

'The Scarecrow could do worse things. Imagine if it put your crystal into the machine and sucked *that* dry. How much power would it get from a being as old and powerful as the Golem of Omus?'

Ros's creeping dismay became cold fright at the thought. 'It's not going to eat Escher!'

'It will,' said Pukje, 'if we give it the chance.'

Ros was too appalled by the suggestion to maintain two charms at once. The image of Pukje flickered and faded. He forced himself to keep his emotions under control, which was hard because he didn't know what they were precisely. The mixture was too complex and volatile to easily unpick.

At that moment, the flavour of a familiar mind reappeared in the world and his concentration was completely destroyed.

Adi had returned.

For an instant he was back in his body. He had arms and legs, and a runny nose that he didn't have time to wipe. Then his mind was rushing out of the cage to where Adi was.

She stood beside Manton in the stand of trees where they had left Leda and Know-it-All. They were talking.

Ros didn't think. He just burst into her mind like a firework.

'You made it!'

She jumped so violently she made Know-it-All shy away. Manton grabbed the camel's reins and Bronhill made shushing motions with her tiny hands.

'Ros, is that you?' She turned around, looking for him.

'Sorry to give you such a start.' He was genuinely contrite. 'Just talk normally. I'll hear you.'

'Where are you?' she asked. 'Are you all right?'

'I'm still on the island with Varis. The Scarecrow will release me if I let it keep the crystal.' He studied her from afar. She looked exhausted and filthy, with a new layer of slime plastered over the one that had already dried to her skin and clothes. 'Have you only just got back there?'

'I had to wait in the pipe until the tide went out,' she said, pulling a face that captured much better than words how dreadful that had been. 'It felt like ages. Now I really need a bath.'

'We'll get you cleaned up right away,' said Manton. 'You're scaring Leda.'

Relief was written large across Adi's face. 'I'm glad this is almost over.'

'It's not over,' said Ros.

'Why do you say that?' she asked.

'The Scarecrow wants to eat Escher.'

He explained what he had seen as quickly as he could. When he had finished, Adi looked puzzled.

'Isn't that a good thing?' she asked. 'The Golem of

Omus will soon be dead, so we can all go back to Samimi and get on with finding Tally Wiskins, completing our trade deal and going home.'

'But that's not what I want. Well, not like this. It just seems wrong.'

'To let the golem be eaten?' Her incredulity was growing. 'Think of what he did to you, Ros. Think of what he made you do! It's the least he deserves.'

'Pukje doesn't want me to do it. I think he's worried about the Scarecrow getting too strong.'

'Who cares what Pukje thinks, or how strong the Scarecrow is? It's none of our business. Let them argue about that after we're gone. Take the Scarecrow's deal, Ros. I don't see what all the fuss is about.'

'It doesn't feel right,' he said.

'There's nothing wrong with the golem dying. Don't tell me you're having second thoughts!'

He couldn't answer that. Now it came to it, maybe he was. Escher had once been a friend. Throwing him away was one thing, but allowing him to be eaten by a creature like the Scarecrow was quite another. What would that make Ros if he let that happen?

Before he could think of a way to express those thoughts, he felt Adi's mind shift. It was a subtle thing, like noticing that someone had lost interest in a conversation before it had ended. She looked the same, but her thoughts were elsewhere.

'How are you talking to me?' she asked him.

'Through the Change,' he said.

'Your voice sounds like it's in my head. Is that where you are?'

'I guess. I don't really know —'

'Can you see what I'm thinking?'

Now he began to feel anxious. 'It doesn't work that way, Adi.'

'Then how does it work, Ros? Tell me.'

'I learned the charm from Mage Shurven. She didn't really explain.'

'You're not doing a very good job of it either.' She sounded hurt. 'Is this how you knew about the lullaby, Ros? Have you been reading my mind?'

He wanted to reassure her, but the words wouldn't come. Maybe he *could* read her mind, if he wanted. Maybe there was no limit to the power his ability with the Change could give him. If that was the case, maybe she had a right to be angry. He possessed knowledge about her she no longer wanted to share.

'Adi —'

It was too late. With all the force of a slamming door, she put the charm back on and vanished from his sight.

He returned to his body in despair. Someone was shaking his shoulder. It seemed to have been going on for some time.

'Snap out of it, boy,' Quirk was saying. 'Your time is up.'

'What?' Ros blinked up into the man's bloodshot eyes. Quirk was bending over him, inside the cage. 'Time for what?'

'To make up your mind. Do you know what you want in exchange for the crystal? My master needs to know, and he doesn't like to be kept waiting.'

Ros thought fast. Pukje's words whispered from one corner of his mind while Adi whispered from another. One wanted him to save Escher while the other was happy to consign the golem to his grisly fate.

He needed time to think, and there was only one sure way to get that.

'I'm not leaving here without the crystal,' he said. 'Tell your master it needs to come up with a different deal.'

Quirk pulled back, a severe expression on his face. He left the cage and closed the door behind him. Without a word, he stomped through the rattling web and disappeared through the nearest door.

Ros lay back against Varis, who still hadn't moved, and closed his eyes. He had just committed himself to fighting both the Scarecrow and Adi, and he didn't know which one to fear the most.

5

Enter a Dragon

Tap tap tap. So went the pebble at the end of Pukje's thread within minutes of Quirk's departure. Ros ignored the irritation even though it was concentrated right between his eyes. He too was concentrating, on following Quirk's progress through the jumble of buildings and into the Scarecrow's laboratory. The man walked quickly and muttered unintelligibly to himself along the way. Occasionally he slapped an open palm against his thigh as though urging himself to go faster.

When he reached the laboratory, he knocked and waited for the order to enter. He left the door open behind him. He obviously thought there was no one else in the fort who might spy on what took place within.

Ros's point of view was unable to cross the threshold but he had a perfect line of sight through the open door. The Scarecrow was working on the tangle of new charms, rearranging its parts into something resembling symmetry. The machine designed to devour Escher was obviously incomplete. Two gaps remained that would need to be filled before the Scarecrow would be ready to begin its work on the golem. At the rate it was working, those gaps might not be empty for long.

'The boy declines your offer,' said Quirk, bowing low. 'He is stubborn and wilful.'

'Gahh,' hissed the Scarecrow in annoyance. 'Strength makes him confident beyond all reason. Such is the way with humans.'

'What will we do now, Master? We can't just let him go.'

'Indeed. That would be inequitable and dangerous. Without an agreement between us, who knows what he might reveal? And we cannot simply kill them now because the girl-thing escaped. We *must* reach an agreement.'

'What would you have me do, Master?'

'The boy-thing's mind is clearly addled. Bring me the man-thing instead. Perhaps we can reason with him.'

'But he is unconscious.'

'Find a way to wake him, then.' One sharp-tipped hand waved in irritation. 'Go, go! You disturb my concentration.'

Quirk bowed and left the laboratory.

Ros opened his eyes and reached up to take the dangling pebble. There would be a short time to talk before Quirk returned.

(Tell me how to break the charm around the Scarecrow's laboratory,) he said as soon as the connection was open between him and Pukje.

(Why?)

(So I can keep my side of our bargain.)

(All right, but it's not easy. The Scarecrow's barrier is a very old one and is in constant use. It's as much a part of the laboratory as the stone in the walls, and would be as hard to break. The trick is to make a window.)

(How big?)

(Not nearly big enough for you fit through, I'm afraid. Maybe the size of an apple.)

Ros considered Pukje's answer for a long time.

Pukje interpreted his silence as disappointment. (I'm sorry, Ros,) he said. (That's all I can tell you. I don't know everything.)

Ros looked up, struck again by the contrast between Pukje and Escher. Where one had claimed ignorance on no subject at all and yet withheld the truth at every opportunity, the other made no bones about his fallibility and had yet to lead him astray once.

(No, that's enough,) Ros said. (Show me how to do it.)

Pukje captured the essence of the trick in a few short sentences, which he repeated calmly and patiently when Ros had difficulty following some of the details. It was a charm like no other he had performed: multi-layered and subtle, a match for the artistry the Scarecrow had performed on his most private lair. Ros didn't dare doubt that he could pull it off. His need was absolute; he had to have the confidence to match.

Quirk returned just as Ros thought he had the charm memorised. He let go of the pebble and Pukje hastily pulled it up into the shadows. Quirk tinkered with the lock and warned Ros to stay back. He obeyed, not wanting to raise any alarms at this point. There would be plenty later, if he was successful.

Quirk produced a tube of foul-smelling ointment from his robe and waved it under Varis's nose. The Clansman stirred but didn't wake. Quirk gave him another dose, and slapped him twice across the face.

Varis blinked and opened his eyes. 'Where ...?' He clearly didn't remember anything until he saw Ros. With a grunt, he tried to sit up. 'What ...?'

'It's okay. Adi's safe,' Ros told him. 'Go with Quirk. Don't agree to anything.'

'Shut up, you,' said Quirk and hauled Varis to his feet.

The Clansman swayed unsteadily as Quirk helped him out of the cage. There was a moment of awkwardness as Quirk tried to close the door while also keeping Varis upright. Ros only added to his confusion by closing the door for him, then stepping obediently back.

'You're fooling no one,' Quirk said with a scowl.

Ros watched him stagger off, grunting and straining under Varis's weight. As soon as he was out of sight, Ros lay on the floor of the cage with his hands folded across his stomach and sent his mind back to the laboratory.

The Scarecrow was building the second-to-last charm, hunched over a workbench like a strange, predatory bird. Its concentration seemed unbreakable, a fact Ros was going to rely upon. For now, he ignored his captor and focussed on doing everything that Pukje had told him.

The boundary charm around the laboratory would not prevent physical objects passing through it, Pukje had told him, but would raise a ruckus if someone forced it open using the Change. Ros needed to get as close as he could to the barrier's surface without triggering a reaction. There he would spread his point of view flat, like a pancake, and look near rather than far. It had taken Ros a long time to grasp that particular concept. Just as the Scarecrow's mysterious telescope could see powerful artefacts from far away, so too could devices be made that would make small things seem large. Ros had no such device, but he didn't need one. He had the Change. Through it he could search the invisible boundary between him and the inside of the laboratory, looking for a weakness.

Quirk arrived with Varis much sooner than Ros had expected. Time was flying faster than he liked. Redoubling his efforts, he located a tiny dimple that he decided could be enlarged, halfway up the wall to the right of the door. Drawing all his willpower to a point sharper than the keenest needle imaginable, he wormed into the wall by tiny degrees, encouraging the dimple to expand rather than forcing it to. The wall was strong and flexible. All he had to do was make it bend the right way, so it wouldn't break and set off the alarm.

He was concentrating so hard he didn't hear the conversation inside the laboratory. He noted only that Varis sounded defiant and the Scarecrow more than a little peeved. Clearly it wasn't getting from Varis what it had hoped for.

Ros widened and deepened the dimple until it had almost reached the far side of the boundary. One last push and he would be able to enter the laboratory undetected. Far away, his body took a deep breath.

Slowly, carefully, he eased forward.

As gently as water, the barrier melted around him and allowed him inside.

From then on, he wasted no time. He swept his point of view across the room to where the crystal lay on its silver plate. Pausing to remember one of the very earliest charms he had ever learnt, he gathered his concentration and gripped the crystal with his mind as tightly as though he held it in his fist.

There he froze, waiting to be sure that the Scarecrow was sufficiently distracted.

'Your attitude confounds me,' the Scarecrow was saying. 'You are the adult. You make the decisions. That is how human societies are supposed to work. Yet you willingly relinquish your authority to someone considerably your junior in age and status. Are you considered abnormal?'

'I don't know what *you* are,' Varis said, 'but you've got a lot to learn about people.' Although he leaned against the nearest workbench for support, he held his head high. 'If Ros doesn't want you to have his crystal, then I say you shouldn't have it. It doesn't matter if I disagree with him; it's his business, not mine. Adi is safe. That's where my duty lies.'

'Absurd!' The Scarecrow paced back and forth in front of Varis, the green of its eyes flickering and flaring. 'The illogic of your argument is impenetrable! Quirk, can you find a way to convince him of his error?'

Judging that the three of them were completely preoccupied, Ros flexed his will and lifted the crystal up into the air. It seemed to weigh nothing, yet controlling it was as difficult as balancing a rock on the head of a pin. Ros was juggling so many charms at once that he feared the whole lot would crash down. That would literally mean dropping the crystal and he could not, under any circumstances, allow that to happen. Just because he didn't want Escher to be eaten didn't mean he wanted a liberated golem on his hands.

Up, up, up the crystal went. Originally he had intended simply to hide it in the rafters, but seeing Pukje peering through the chink in the ceiling, overseeing his efforts, gave Ros a better idea. Swinging it towards the little man's outstretched hands, he gratefully handed it over to someone else for safekeeping.

Pukje didn't immediately disappear into the shadows. First he raised an object and waved it in order to attract Ros's attention. It was a light-coloured stone similar in size and shape to the crystal. Not so similar that it would fool anyone looking closely, but enough perhaps for a casual glance to slide over it.

Grateful for Pukje's forethought, Ros took the stone and lowered it gently down from the roof and onto the silver plate. The Scarecrow was still arguing with Varis. Its impatience to get back to work was barely disguised.

Ros slipped unnoticed to Varis and spoke directly into the Clansman's mind.

'Don't be startled. Don't say anything at all. Just listen to me.'

Varis's eyes widened slightly, but apart from that he didn't react.

'I've got the crystal. We can leave now. Tell the Scarecrow you've changed your mind and we'll take the deal.'

With a barely perceptible nod, Varis acknowledged the instruction.

Satisfied that he had done everything he could, Ros retreated to the hole in the laboratory's protective barrier. He reversed the procedure he had followed before, easing himself through the hole and closing it behind him, leaving only the faintest of scars in his wake.

He didn't stick around to listen to Varis announce his change of heart, although he could imagine the Scarecrow's relief and Quirk's puzzlement. His distant head was aching, and with some relief he snapped back to his body and relaxed his grip on the Change. The crystal was out of the Scarecrow's clutches. That was a step in the right direction. Now all they had to do was escape.

With the last of his energy he wiped his nose. Blood, again. He had come close to overexerting himself a second time that day.

He didn't realise that he had fallen asleep until the tapping of the pebble on his face woke him up.

(The golem's prison is safe,) Pukje told him. (The charm that hides me from the Scarecrow's telescope is keeping it hidden too.)

(Thanks,) said Ros. He barely had the energy to hold the pebble. (You will give it back to me, won't you?)

(Of course I will. It's yours. You named it; you own it.)

That triggered a thought that hadn't occurred to Ros before. (If I rename Escher, would that stop the Scarecrow eating him?)

(I'm afraid not,) Pukje said. (For a start, you can't rename something once it's been named properly. That's just the way things work. Also, the Scarecrow isn't trying to control the golem, he's planning to siphon its power, so names aren't required. If we needed to know the name of everything we ate, we'd never get through a meal.)

Ros nodded. (All right.)

(Quirk is on his way back with Varis. The Scarecrow has instructed him to let you both go.)

(I can't wait,) Ros said, letting his eyes sink closed again.

Now that Escher had been retrieved, his thoughts turned to patching things up with Adi. He had to find a way to convince her that he would do nothing to cause her harm. Apart from Know-it-All, she was his only friend in the whole world.

Pukje was saying something, but Ros couldn't concentrate. Why was he so tired? It wasn't just because of the charms he had so recently been using. This was something different. His limbs had been aching for weeks, and he was constantly hungry. The thought made his stomach rumble noisily, reminding him that he hadn't eaten since their meal on the road the previous morning.

The sound of Quirk and Varis making their way through the web roused him. He sat up and prepared to look annoyed by the news.

'We're leaving,' said Varis, playing the part perfectly. 'I've told the Scarecrow it can keep the crystal.'

'What? You can't do that!'

'I can, and there's no point arguing about it. My mind is made up. On your feet, Ros. We can't lie around here forever.'

Ros feigned disgruntlement for Quirk's sharp eyes and dragged his heels out of the cage. It was hard not to break into a run now that he knew freedom was just moments away. He couldn't seem too eager.

Quirk led them through the fort along a route Ros had not followed before. The corridors were windowless, cool and dry, leading steadily downwards via stairs and curved ramps. Once they took a right turn past a large number of empty storage and guest rooms. The wing might have been a barracks some time in the past. There was enough space to house a small army.

When the floor beneath them flattened out, Ros assumed they had reached something approaching ground level. That assumption was confirmed when they passed a series of small stables, one of which held a scruffy-looking mule, and came at last to a large double-door, twice as high as Varis, that stood directly in their path. Ros could smell sea-water on the far side, and even hear gulls squawking at each other with their rude voices. A handful of steps and they would be free.

Quirk fished under his robe for a large key, which he slotted into a lock of matching proportions but didn't immediately turn. 'You must never come back here,' he told them. 'My master is very literal-minded. If you break the deal, there's no telling what it might do.'

'Don't worry,' Varis said. 'Wild camels couldn't drag me back.'

'Will you promise not to come after us again?' Ros asked.

'Why would we? We have what we want.'

'I hope it's enough,' said Varis. 'I hope it'll keep your master happy.'

Quirk licked his lips. A flicker of emotion passed across his face that Ros couldn't quite read. Just for a second it looked as though Quirk was going to ask if he could come with them too.

Then the sound of a distant shriek reached them, reverberating through the island like a tornado building up to full strength.

Quirk looked at Varis and Ros with shock and betrayal in his eyes. His right hand tightened around the key while his left slipped back under his robes, reaching for a charm.

Before Quirk could do more than that, Varis drew back his right fist and punched him hard on the chin. Quirk didn't stagger. He simply dropped like a puppet with its strings cut, eyes rolled up into his head.

Varis stepped back, rubbing his hand.

There was no time for congratulation. The shrieking was growing louder and closer. Varis wrenched the key in the massive lock, and Ros looked nervously behind them, half-expecting to see the Scarecrow thundering down the corridor already. For the moment, it was empty.

With a series of heavy clunks, the lock turned. A crack of light appeared between the two doors. Ros helped Varis push them open, and grabbed the key as they slipped through. They were in another long tunnel, this one carved from the naked rock and leading down to the stony island shore. Ros helped Varis close the door behind them and waited until it was locked again. Then they were hurrying down the sloping tunnel towards the bright light of day, Ros doing his best to keep up with Varis's loping stride. Their speed picked up as the end approached. Ros actually ran the last few metres, forgetting his exhaustion and sprinting to freedom.

What he saw at the end of the tunnel shocked him.

Water roiled and foamed around the hungry rocks. Their route to freedom was covered by the tide.

'Now what?' he asked, hoping Varis would have the answer.

'I can't swim. Can you?'

'No.'

Behind them, something heavy slammed into the door.

Varis swallowed. 'I think we're going to have to try.'

They picked their way across the rocks until they were out of sight from the door and as close to the cliffs as they could get. Ros looked for Adi but there was no sign of her. Perhaps it was better that she wasn't there, he thought. All she could have done was watch.

The crashing on the door was louder than the waves as Ros and Varis stepped down into the water. It was bracingly cold but not as icy as he had feared. Currents swept around them, tugging their balance backwards and forwards. Taking great care not to slip on the rocks, Ros descended as far as his waist, and then watched to see what Varis would do next. The Clansman looked pale and much more nervous than he had been confronting the Scarecrow.

Taking a deep breath, Varis jumped off the edge of his rock and give himself up completely to the water.

He didn't go under. He barely even got his shoulders wet. With a relieved and startled look, he turned to Ros and said, 'I can touch the bottom!'

Ros found that he had stopped breathing without knowing it. Following Varis's lead, he jumped forward and reached for the seabed. It was there, at the tip of his questing toes. His chin was barely above water, but he could breathe. Perhaps they could make it after all.

The going was slow. Every step was a war against the weight of the sea, with waves surging up unexpectedly and occasionally ditching over him. At least, he thought, he would be cleaner when he reached the cliffs. Maybe that would help Adi like him again.

'Behind us!' Varis called over the sound of the surf.

Only then did Ros realise that the crashing on the door had stopped. He turned just in time to see the Scarecrow step out of the tunnel and turn its green-eyed head from side to side, hissing like an overstressed boiler.

'Duck under!' Varis cried, but it was too late. The creature had seen them. Walking with high, careful steps, it negotiated the rocks directly in front of the tunnel mouth and approached the water.

Ros hoped it wouldn't be able to enter the sea, but the Scarecrow waded in without hesitation and moved quickly after them.

He kicked vainly against the sandy sea-bottom. It was hard to find traction. Waving his arms achieved something, but he knew he was going too slowly. In seconds the Scarecrow had halved the distance between them, its weight and strength more than a match for human endurance. Malignant green eyes were firmly fixed on him.

Then something dropped from the sky like a giant bird, flapping mighty wings to bring it up just before plunging into the sea. The Scarecrow reared back on seeing it, screeching loud enough to deafen Ros. Gnarled claws unfurled from two muscular legs and clutched at the Scarecrow, sending it rearing back even further. The snapping of wings created powerful downdraughts that flattened the waves and sent spray into Ros's eyes.

'Back, you fiend!' roared the Scarecrow, recovering from its surprise. 'The boy-thing is mine!'

It snatched at the gnarled claws with metal claws of its own, and the winged shape retreated into the sky.

'Back, back!' the Scarecrow bellowed.

'No!' Ros cried, although he could see the effort required to hang motionless in the air like that.

With one last straining flap, the winged shape ascended and flew off around the curve of the island. Whatever it had been, whoever had sent it, it was no help to them.

Desperately, Ros put all his thought and effort into moving forward, away from the Scarecrow. He kept his eyes on the cliffs, willing them to come closer. The Change stirred at the wish, but his strength was still sapped by the exertion of getting through the barrier and stealing the crystal. He could no more fight their way free than swim.

Behind them the Scarecrow huffed and splashed, showing no sign of slowing down. Surely, thought Ros, it had to run out of the Change some time. That was the only hope he had left.

It was soon dashed. The Scarecrow caught up with them and lunged with sharp-tipped hands upraised.

Varis hurled himself at the thing and managed to overbalance it. They both went under, and emerged a second later, spluttering and splashing. Ros ducked as the Scarecrow lunged for him. The sea-water caught in his throat, nose and ears. His eyes stung. A froth of bubbles and sand effectively blinded him. He stayed down as long as he could but the burning in his lungs could not be resisted. With a gasp, he launched himself upwards.

And kept going.

Ros cried out in surprise as a shadow fell over him and strong talons gripped his shoulders. Powerful wings flapped twice. With a surge of strength, the giant bird-creature that had harried the Scarecrow before pulled him out of the water and wheeled about to fly him away.

'Why are you doing this?' Ros shouted at the creature's leathery underbelly. It had no feathers, just rough skin that stretched across its wings to the point of transparency. If it had a voice, it didn't use it.

'What about Varis? We can't leave him behind!'

The wings flapped on. Ros twisted to look below and behind him. Already Varis and the Scarecrow were tiny, reduced by height and distance to miniatures of themselves. He could still hear the Scarecrow's furious shrieking, although it was getting fainter by the second.

'I'm not leaving without Varis!' Ros wriggled in the unyielding grip. 'Take me back!'

The flying beast grunted as though in annoyance and tipped its wings to take them around the island. They circled it, avoiding its ragged ramparts and spire. Ros was giddy with speed and height. His shouts died in his throat. His breath had been completely taken away.

The cliffs hove back into view, followed by Varis and the Scarecrow. They had barely moved. Ros felt his stomach rise up in his chest as his would-be rescuer stopped flapping and lost height. The water came up to meet them. Ros almost regretted his decision when the claws loosed him and sent him falling into the waves.

He hit with a splash and came up gasping. The flying beast had dropped him a dozen metres from the Scarecrow, near the tunnel entrance. Immediately the Scarecrow started back towards him, eyes flaring in anger. Varis followed, and Ros wanted to scream in frustration. What was he doing? This was his chance to escape!

It occurred to him that Varis might have thought exactly the same thing just moments ago, about him. They would escape together, or not at all.

The flying creature vanished behind the island once more. This time it didn't reappear.

The Scarecrow loomed over Ros, angular and furious. 'Why have you returned, boy-thing?' it grated. 'To honour your bargain or to further my enemy's sabotage?'

'I made no bargain with you,' Ros said, wincing as its metal fingers clutched him, 'or your enemy. I don't even know what that thing was.'

'The dragon has plagued me for generations. I would be rid of it, and soon.'

The Scarecrow wheeled about as Varis approached. 'You cannot harm me,' it told him. 'Desist, oath-breaker.'

'Let's just get out of the water,' said Ros. He was beginning to shiver.

The Scarecrow tugged him bodily through the salty spume, and Varis followed. Quirk was waiting for them on the stony shore, dried blood on his mouth and a murderous look in his eyes. Varis climbed out without help, and the two men sized each other up from a respectful distance.

'You don't have the crystal,' Varis said, 'and neither do we. We're useless to you. Why don't you let us go?'

'You know where it is,' said Quirk. 'We'll find out eventually.'

'Enough,' the Scarecrow told them both. 'The enemy is here, a circumstance that calls for desperate measures and a new arrangement. I am beset with possibilities.'

The machine-creature handed Ros to Quirk. Its eyes were flickering on and off. Finally, much too late, fatigue seemed to be catching up with it.

'To the laboratory,' it said. 'We will talk there. I give you my word, boy-thing ...' Gears ground inside its domed skull. '... I mean, *Roslin*, that you will come to no immediate harm.'

The use of his full name was clearly intended as a sign of respect. That, combined with its weird understanding of honour, was enough to convince Ros that the Scarecrow was sincere about its unexpected change of heart. What new arrangement could it be talking about? Ignoring Quirk's intense animosity, he followed the lumbering machine back up the ramp and into the island. Their escape plan had been foiled, but fate, it seemed, was about to surprise them once again.

6

The Promise of Youth

The Scarecrow might have professed to be open to discussion, but Quirk wasn't in a forgiving mood. When Ros stumbled, the man pushed at him, forcing him to keep up despite his shorter legs. Ros's wet clothes were heavy and chilling. By the time they reached the laboratory, he had stopped dripping but his teeth were still chattering.

'Bring them towels,' the Scarecrow instructed Quirk. 'Food and water, also. They have gone without long enough.'

The reluctant assistant hurried off to obey his orders, nursing his bruised jaw, while the Scarecrow connected itself by a glowing string to the main green cable. Its eyes returned to normal and its movements regained their usual vigour, but the cable itself was looking much dimmer than it had the day before. Its light barely cast a shadow now.

Ros glanced up at the ceiling, but could see nothing to indicate that Pukje was watching.

Quirk returned with two rough towels, a hunk of

cheese and some crusts of bread. Ros was more interested in the jug of brackish water, which he and Varis shared. He had swallowed a gutful of sea-water and been left thirstier for it. Gradually the craving passed and he was able to think about other things.

As Ros ate, he watched the Scarecrow pace the circumference of the laboratory, studying the walls through a blue magnifying glass and occasionally tapping at it with a tuning fork that never seemed to sound the same pitch. Finally it stopped at a point near the door and rapped the stone with its knuckles.

'Here,' it said. 'This is where you entered when you stole the crystal.'

Ros imagined himself standing on the other side of the door, looking for a weak point. That seemed about the right place. 'When I stole it back, you mean.'

'So you admit you did it.' The Scarecrow swivelled its torso and head to stare at him without moving its feet. It had never looked as inhuman as it did at that moment. 'The theft wasn't the work of my enemy — unless you are in league with each other against me.'

Ros still didn't know anything about the Scarecrow's enemy — unless it had something to do with Pukje. It seemed safer for the moment to assume all responsibility for the act.

'No,' he said around a mouthful of bread and cheese, 'it was just me.'

The Scarecrow's legs and feet moved then, bringing its waist around and walking it closer to where Ros sat with Varis on stools Quirk had provided.

'Remarkable,' it said. Its eyes never left him once. 'You are much more resourceful than I believed a human child could be. When I heard of your achievements from Quirk, I thought them exaggerations. The Golem of Omus was all that mattered.'

'They are exaggerations,' Ros said, abruptly losing his appetite.

'And yet the golem was contained. Are you telling me that was not your doing?'

He couldn't deny it, even though the idea had been inspired by Mage Shurven, the man'kin called Vasoph, and even Escher himself. 'I guess I did do that,' he admitted.

'Define the line between truth and fable for me, then,' said the Scarecrow. 'Did you not also defeat the Bee Witch?'

'Sort of.'

'A new lake has formed in the northern desert. Is that your work too?'

Ros had to think hard about that one. He remembered a Sky Warden charm that he had smashed in the Bee Witch's lair, prompting a flood. If it was still flowing, that water could well have formed a lake.

'I didn't mean to do that,' he said. 'It was an accident.'

'Such accidents don't happen to ordinary people, Roslin of Geheb. The stories also tell of a girl-thing bitten by crabblers and brought back to life. I believe I glimpsed her earlier. Your friend's aura was that of someone touched by the Void.'

'Yes, that was her,' Ros said with a pang of concern. What was Adi doing now? Was she cursing him for getting Varis into trouble or thinking he wasn't trying hard enough to get the Clansman off the island?

'The stories go on. Befriending the man'kin of Jakati, navigating the Weird, defeating an experienced golem-hunter, battling a crabbler coven —'

'All right, all right.' Ros raised his hands. 'It was me, most of it, but only with a lot of help. I couldn't have done it on my own.'

'None of the people who helped you could have done anything on their own,' said the Scarecrow, tilting its head to one side. 'Think on that, as I am thinking on it.'

Ros frowned. There didn't seem anything to consider. 'I don't understand.'

The Scarecrow finally broke its intense examination of him and walked around the workbenches towards the tangle of charms it had been building.

Ros and Varis exchanged looks of mutual puzzlement.

'My latest device is finished,' the Scarecrow announced. 'With it, I would have devoured the Golem of Omus and by that means ensured my survival for many years. Freed from the fear of starvation, I could have achieved great things. I have dreams, Roslin of Geheb, dreams you could not begin to understand.' Its gaze tracked lovingly across the machine's complicated lines. 'Yet, for all my dreams, I know that I have reached the limit of my ingenuity. I will never build a device greater than this. And without a golem to fuel it, my work will stand idle. Like myself, the thing it was built to do will go undone. The dust will settle on us both, and over long aeons smother us completely.'

Ros was no closer to understanding. 'Where do I come into this, exactly?'

'I will never achieve anything greater than this,' the Scarecrow repeated, twisting unnaturally to face him again, 'unless you help me do it.'

Ros straightened. 'What?'

'Since my first proposition is unacceptable, I offer you a new one. Become my apprentice and I will teach you all I know. In you I sense a mind that has only begun to hunger for greatness. With my guidance, you will stand tall among your fellows. Together we will achieve our destinies.'

Ros didn't know what to say. Varis glanced between him and the Scarecrow with equal parts worry and suspicion.

Quirk reacted negatively too. 'Master, think carefully. The boy is untrustworthy. Has he not proven that many times over?'

'He has,' said the Scarecrow, 'but it is clear he feels that we have treated him unjustly. Perhaps he was right to fight us.'

'How can it be right, Master? It is wrong to defy you.'

'My original negotiations were conducted on assumptions that later turned out to be incorrect. This boy-thing has advanced significantly in the course of his pursuits. Immature he is, yes, but he has potential to become a more superior being than the ordinary human. He has the promise of youth beyond measure. Roslin of Geheb is the prize, not the thing he carried.'

'At your side,' said Ros, 'working with you, together?'

The Scarecrow nodded. 'What say you?'

'Master —'

'Be silent, Quirk. I will hear no more from you on this subject.'

Quirk shut his mouth, looking like he was trying very hard not to be sick.

'What do I say?' Ros repeated.

For a long minute, he didn't know what was going through his mind. Mage Shurven and Mister Alembic had both spoken of his need for a teacher. This could be the very opportunity he had been looking for, even though it came from such an unexpected angle. While the thought of being trapped on the island with the Scarecrow and his jealous assistant wasn't a pleasant one, wasn't it worth considering if it helped Varis get away? Perhaps later, if things didn't work out, he could escape from the island himself, to seek out Adi and the others and begin his life anew.

But uncertainties plagued him. The success of the plan depended entirely on being able to find Adi. Even if he did manage to heal the rift between them, she was just one person out of many in a very large world. Adi would never stay put and wait for him. She wanted to be a trader, a traveller, like everyone else in her Clan. How could he be sure they would meet again?

And who was to say the Scarecrow would ever be done with him? The longer he stayed, the more indebted he would become, and the more opportunities would arise for the Scarecrow to trap him forever, no matter how he tried to wriggle free.

Humans might seem to the Scarecrow to pass as fleetingly as mayflies, but Ros only had one life. He wasn't going to waste it on something like this.

'I say thank you, but no.'

The Scarecrow's lidless eyes didn't so much as flicker. 'Be sure of your answer. Would you like more time to consider?'

'No. I am sure.'

'Good. Then you cannot say later that I did not give you fair warning.'

With lightning speed, the Scarecrow lunged for him. Knife-like fingers gripped his arms. He struggled but couldn't pull away. The Scarecrow's energies were fully rejuvenated, while Ros's reserves of the Change were still weakened.

'Hold the man-thing!' the machine-creature said to Quirk as it dragged Ros bodily towards a workbench. There, two small charms rested. The largest was L-shaped and clearly designed for a human hand. One arm of the L had a round hole in its end, revealing a tube that ran down its length.

The Scarecrow took one hand off Ros long enough to grip the other end of the charm and press the open hole to his throat. The tip of one finger pressed a small lever. A mechanism clicked, and something stabbed into Ros's neck. He cried out and clutched at the tiny wound.

The Scarecrow threw him to the ground and put the charm to one side. 'There,' it said. 'I should have done this much earlier.'

It picked up the second charm, a tube like a telescope with glass lenses at either end, and pointed one end of the tube at Ros so he could see through it. Visible in its blurry depths was a, dim red glow. 'The light shines brightest when pointing at you,' the Scarecrow explained, turning the tube so the other end was aimed directly at Ros. Red light bathed its face. 'Escape if you must, but know that I will always track you down.'

Ros could feel the thing in his neck burrowing deep, buzzing with the Change like a tiny, flesh-dwelling fly. Strange sensations swept up and down his spine, and for a moment he was completely unable to stand.

'Ros! Are you all right?' Varis called out.

The Scarecrow turned its back on him and went to deal with the Clansman. Quirk had armed himself with a long metal rod and was doing his best to avoid any more punches. Pinned between Quirk and the Scarecrow, Varis didn't stand a chance. Even when he raised a fist to threaten the Scarecrow's masterwork, the machine-creature didn't hesitate. Moving more quickly than a mere human, it caught Varis's arm and stayed it from falling. Then it dragged him well away from anything fragile.

'Take the boy-thing and secure him as best you can,' the Scarecrow instructed Quirk. 'He will not run, I think. He knows that we could find him in short order if he did.'

Quirk hauled Ros to his feet. His legs felt wobbly but they were regaining their strength. Now it was his hands that had lost their usefulness. They flapped at his sides like wet laundry.

Varis went to follow, but the Scarecrow held tightly to his arms. 'No, man-thing, you stay.'

'What do you want with him?' asked Ros. 'It's me you're after.'

'Think of this as punishment for turning down my offer.' The Scarecrow's head dipped low. 'You may be strong, but your cognition leaves much to be desired.'

'It's okay, Ros,' Varis said, belying the disquiet in his eyes. 'I'm happy to be a hostage. We make him nervous, not the other way around.'

The Scarecrow issued a low, rhythmic noise from its chest that might have been laughter. 'You flatter yourself. This has nothing to do with fear or keeping you hostage.'

'Don't you dare hurt him,' shouted Ros, a terrible foreboding rising up inside him. The Scarecrow didn't look as though Ros's decision had taken it by surprise. It looked, in fact, as though it had been expecting events to play out this way.

The machine-creature approached him, dragging Varis after it like a child.

'Hurt?' it said. 'Perhaps I will.'

'If you do anything to him, I'll kill you.' Ros felt his fury rising in step with his desperation. 'I'll find a way and I'll kill you dead.'

'Why? This is your doing, not mine. You stole the crystal. You refused to help me.' Its face came awfully close, just centimetres from Ros's nose. 'You asked earlier where you came into this, Roslin of Geheb. There were in fact two answers to that question. You denied me the first of them. Now I give you the other.' Its free arm pointed like a spear at the cluster of charms. 'My device will not sit idle. It was built to do one thing,

but with a few small adjustments it could do another —
and that other, I now see, is full of so much more
promise. The conclusion is inevitable, is it not?'

The thing's lifeless eyes came closer, turning Ros's
fury to dread.

'From artefact to golem to human,' it said. 'When I
devour Roslin of Geheb, all his promise and potential
will become mine. But first I must test the process, and
that is where the man-thing proves his use. Remove the
boy-thing, Quirk. I can afford no distractions.'

Ros kicked and struggled but couldn't resist Quirk's
superior strength. Varis was equally helpless in the
Scarecrow's hands. Ros could see that he was trying to
remain resolute but not entirely succeeding.

'Don't worry about me, Ros,' Varis called as the door
swung shut. 'Save yourself so you can look after —'

Adi. The name was obscured by the slamming of the
door. How could Ros look after anyone if he was going
to be eaten? The situation was utterly hopeless.

Quirk dragged him in grim silence back to the cage.
There was nothing Ros could do to fight him. He had
tried everything, and here he was, back in captivity again.
The buzzing in his throat had ceased, but he knew the
charm was still there, part of him now, unchangeable.

Roslin of Geheb is the prize ...

The door clanged shut, reinforced with heavy chains
and no fewer than three locks. Quirk was taking no
chances.

'How could you serve a monster like that?' Ros said.

Quirk didn't meet his eye. With one final test of the
chains, he slumped against the bars. 'It hasn't always

been like this,' he said. 'My master keeps journals. I read them sometimes, when it's distracted. I've learned something of its origins.' He did glance at Ros then, as though to make sure he wasn't talking to himself, but looked quickly away again. 'A long time ago, this island was inhabited by an army. The general in charge of the army was so nervous of an approach by sea that he had a machine made — a machine that could scan the horizon day and night, without sleeping or resting, with absolute loyalty. And it did its job, intelligently and thoughtfully, even though an assault never came and the army went to fight elsewhere. The general didn't switch off his machine when he left, and he never returned to do so.

'Decades passed and the machine continued to scan the horizon, taking notes as it went. Time aged it and strained it. It found ways to prolong its operation, cannibalising the other machines on the island, rebuilding itself and making itself more independent. It took the occasional servant from humans who stumbled across the island, one of which gave it the name by which it has called itself ever since. Another taught the Scarecrow how to make new charms to protect itself and its task, despite its forgetting at times what that task really was. The search for the invading army became a search for more artefacts; the notes it took became its journal. Gradually it evolved into the thing you see today — purposeful, full of knowledge, but still a machine at heart. Part of it, I think, a very deep part, is still waiting for the general to return.'

Quirk's eyes met Ros's at last. They were red-rimmed

and exhausted. The skin beneath his beard was inflamed. 'Does that answer your question?'

'But to experiment on people — to kill them —'

'You're the one who started this.' Quirk's voice became hard with anger and derision. 'If you'd just let us have the golem, it would never have come to this.'

'But that's not right either!'

'Why not? It's a golem. It's done worse things.'

Ros hung his head, unable to face Adi's argument again.

Quirk wasn't done. 'Don't you know that it's still doing them? You may have locked it in the crystal, but don't think that's rendered it completely harmless. How have you been feeling lately? My bet is, not very well. The golem is sucking at your life bit by bit. Sucking at your youth. I don't know where you've hidden it, but I suggest you leave it there forever. Carry it around much longer and you'll die before your time.'

Ros raised his head and stared at him. There was no sign at all that Quirk was lying, but the truth was more abominable than he could bear.

'Do you see now how it feels to be loyal to something that hurts you?' Quirk said bitterly.

The green light dimmed and then brightened again.

'My master needs me,' said the man, heading off through the web.

Ros watched him go. There was nothing else he could do.

Quirk returned a timeless interval later with Varis slung over his shoulder like a sack of flour. Grunting, he laid the Clansman on the floor outside the cage, his back against the bars, and left him there without a word. Varis's hands were tied in front of him and his eyes were open. His breathing was regular and slow. He could have been resting but for the fact that he didn't register Ros's presence at all. He had soiled himself too. Ros felt his heart break. The body before him was as empty as a doll's.

Ros crouched with his hands on Varis's shoulders, clutching them gently so he wouldn't tip over. That was the best Ros could do for him. He guessed what was coming but was powerless to stop it. Varis's heart-name was unknown to him and the Scarecrow's machine was far beyond his understanding. Ros could only hold him as the Clansman's breathing steadily slowed and slowed, and then it stopped.

Ros wept, not caring if Quirk caught him at it. It had all been for nothing. Varis had tried his hardest to save them, and he was the one who had fallen. The Scarecrow had killed him, and it was only a matter of time before Quirk returned for Ros. There was nothing to do but wait, remembering how brave Varis had been and knowing that in the end it hadn't made any difference.

Something tapped the back of his neck. He ignored it, but it was insistent. Finally, he reached for the dangling pebble, wiped his eyes and forced himself to sit up straighter.

(The Scarecrow is fine-tuning the machine,) whispered Pukje into his mind. (They're not coming for you immediately.)

(How does that help me?) Ros asked. (I can't run. I can't fight. They might as well come now.)

(Where there's life, there's hope,) Pukje told him. (That's the truth of it, whether you believe it or not.)

To Ros it didn't seem that way at all. Varis was dead. Adi was gone. Know-it-All was far away. The only thing he had left was another voice in his ear, whispering without respite.

(You've had a hard time,) Pukje went on. (Growing up, I mean. There's no denying that. You've seen darker times than most. That's why you're famous. People are at their best when times are most desperate. But when people tell the stories about you, they forget about the cost. They don't know or care about that. I want you to know, Ros, that I know and care, and that I think you astonishingly brave for it. Your bravery is more important than what you can do with the Change.)

Ros took a deep, shuddering breath. (I don't feel like I'm doing anything special.)

(In my experience, special people never do.)

Pukje said nothing for a while, and Ros was glad for the silence. He had time to think about all the things he'd seen and done — and the people he'd met too, like Adi, who had trusted him almost from the beginning, and Mage Shurven, who had given her life in an attempt to save him. The man'kin Vasoph had given him a name, and Yury had given him friendship when it had been most needed. Even Manton, for his own reasons, had gone out of his way to help him and Adi through what had seemed then their darkest hour.

He thought of what Quirk had said: *Do you see now how it feels to be loyal to something that hurts you?*

It would be easy, he thought, to give in to that hurt and let it consume him. But the sacrifices of those he had met forbade it. They wouldn't let him. His memory of them wouldn't let him. Even if he never saw Adi and Know-it-All ever again, even if Varis was dead, their faith in him lived on.

It's sucking at your life bit by bit, Quirk had said of the golem. *Sucking at your youth.*

No wonder he had been tired. No wonder he ached so much. He was old before his time.

Still, he remained glad that he'd rescued the golem from the Scarecrow. Escher deserved much worse than death. He deserved to go to the bottom of the ocean for eternity, as Ros had originally planned — to lie trapped there, driven mad by the futile hope of escape. Not just for what he had done to Ros, but for all the victims that had come before him. He deserved to be punished.

(How are you feeling, Ros?)

(A little better,) he said. (Thank you.)

(Don't thank me yet. I have bad news.)

Ros almost laughed. (What could be worse than this?)

(It's not over yet,) Pukje said.

(I know. I have to escape, for a start.) That escaping would be easier without Varis was a cruel thought he could not suppress.

(That's not sufficient now, Ros. You have something else to do as well, something absolutely critical. You have to destroy the Scarecrow.)

Ros looked up into the shadowy rafters. (*What?*)

(Think about it. The artefacts the Scarecrow usually feeds on are not plentiful; they'll run out no matter how many caged golems or talented young boys it can find. If the Scarecrow's going to last forever, it needs a more reliable source of food. And now it's found one: humans. You and Varis might be the first victims, but do you think it'll stop there? Travellers on the coastal road will be next, then people who live on nearby farms, perhaps even Samimi itself.) Pukje's voice was urgent and insistent. (The new machine the Scarecrow has built will make it more powerful and murderous than ever. It must be stopped. You are the only one who can do that, by destroying it once and for all.)

Ros was dizzy with the thought of it: both the bleak vision Pukje had painted and the task he was supposed to perform. (How on earth am I supposed to do that?)

(There must be a way. All we have to do is find it. Are you recovered from your exertions?)

Ros tested the Change. Some of his ability was returning, but he wasn't strong enough to take on Quirk, let alone the Scarecrow. (Not yet,) he said. (If we knew how long we had ...)

(There's no way of knowing that, unfortunately. I can't be two places at once.)

(What about that dragon thing?)

(No use in here, I'm afraid. We need something else.)

Ros thought hard but came up blank. (It's no good! There's nothing we can do without help, and where's that help going to come from? We're all alone out here. There's no one else. It's hopeless.)

Even as he said that, he felt a familiar tingling through his extended senses. Forgetting Pukje, he reached with his mind out to the cliffs, where he had last made contact with Adi. If she was still there, and if she was talking to him, perhaps there was still a chance.

But she wasn't there. The cliffs were empty — of her or anyone else. There was only one lonely horse tied to a tree, cropping listlessly at the grass.

He looked closer. The horse was Leda, which meant the others had to be around somewhere. But where?

Suspicion flared and turned into alarm. What had Manton done?

The tingle came again. He pursued it instantly, and found the source much closer than he had expected, in a completely different direction. Adi wasn't on the cliffs at all. She was in the water on the other side of the island.

'Adi?' It was still a strain throwing his voice that far, but he wasn't going to let anything stop him. Given a choice between seeing her and talking to her, he chose the latter. 'Are you all right?'

'Better than that.' She sounded defiantly cheerful. 'We're coming to rescue you.'

'Who's we?'

'All of us.'

'Manton too?'

'Of course. You and Varis are doing such a bad job of setting yourselves free. We figured you needed a hand.'

'Varis —' He was unable to say any more. Just then wasn't the time to give her the awful news.

'Are you in a boat or something?' he asked her.

'Or something. Did you know camels can swim? I didn't.'

'You're on Know-it-All?'

'Being pulled along by him, actually. Manton says that was the mistake we made the first time: leaving our most powerful ally behind. If we'd had him, nothing would've gone wrong.'

'He'd never have fit up that pipe.'

'That's why I'm calling. We need another way in. Night's falling, and climbing up the sides of the fort doesn't appeal. Quirk must get his mule in somehow.'

'There's a side entrance to the east. You can't miss it.'

'Thanks. I presume there's a door of some kind.'

'Yes. I can try to open it when you get there.'

'Okay. I'm going to put the charm back on now, just in case anyone's looking. Manton's touching it too, so he's hidden as well. I'll take it off when we arrive.'

Good thinking, Ros thought, remembering the sleeping charm he'd brushed by accident in Varis's cell. 'Don't take too long,' he said. 'I really need you right now.'

'Well, that's your own fault, Ros. Why didn't you tell me I gave you those memories of my own free will? If you hadn't waited for me to remember, I would've been here hours ago.'

Ros was simultaneously pleased and dismayed by her words. She didn't hate him, but Varis might still be alive if he'd been more direct in dealing with the problem.

Some of his internal turmoil must have communicated to Adi through the Change.

'Hey,' she said, 'it's okay. We got here as fast as we could. The tide slowed us down, and getting your big friend down the cliff wasn't easy either. Now it's time to finish this. I hope you're okay with that, because I definitely am.'

She cut the link between them, and Ros sagged in gratitude and relief. He felt a twinge of guilt for mistrusting Manton. Whatever their new friend was up to, he'd had plenty of opportunities to betray them so far and had taken none of them. Ros was now certain that Adi was completely safe with him.

(Who was that?) asked Pukje.

(Adi. She's on her way with Manton and Know-it-All, and Bronhill too, I guess.) He pictured the strange expedition gamely struggling through the waves. It lightened his spirits immeasurably. (I don't know what they're going to do when they get here, but at least I won't be alone.)

(Exactly, Ros. What did I tell you? There's always hope.)

The tension in the thread vanished. It drifted down over him, looping and curling. Pukje followed, scampering lightly and easily through the metal stanchions of the web, barely making it shift under his negligible weight. When he landed next to the cage, he ran up to the bars and reached through them to take Ros's hand.

'If there's one thing I hate,' said the strange little man, 'it's being proven wrong. Now, let's get you out of here. How are you feeling?'

'Still weak,' Ros said, eyeing the cage door uneasily.

'Don't worry about the Change,' Pukje said, pulling a set of slender instruments from under his mossy clothes. 'I'll pick the lock. You conserve your strength. We'll need every bit of it for when the time is right.' He winked. 'I was actually asking about your legs. Do you think you can run?'

Ros nodded. 'Yes, but the Scarecrow can track me wherever I run to.'

'That's why it's so important for you to get out of that cage. Look at the cable; see how dim it's getting? Nothing will wear out our metal friend faster than a good, long chase.'

7

Too Much of a Good Thing

Ros and Pukje had to wait until Adi appeared again before they could tell her the plan. Fortunately, there was no sign of Quirk. The web was silent apart from a slight creaking and groaning as the fort shifted around it. Ros hoped there would be time to get everyone ready before the Scarecrow finished fine-tuning its machine. In the meantime, it was difficult to stay near the cage with poor Varis. Ros laid him flat and folded his arms across his chest. His expression was peaceful.

'The Clan burn their dead,' he told Pukje, 'and scatter their ashes to the desert winds.'

The little man nodded. 'The people of the Strand do the same.'

'Not everyone. We saw a graveyard in Samimi on the way here.'

'I know. Those were memorials only. The bodies were never there.'

Ros looked at him closely. 'How do you know that?'

'I'm interested in dead things.'

'No, how did you know we were at the graveyard?'

Pukje smiled mysteriously, and Ros remembered the bird that had been sailing high above them that day and his feeling of being watched.

Before he could ask any more questions, he sensed Adi take off the charm. He immediately sent himself to her through the Change, using two charms at once. His strength was returning, along with his confidence. With her around, things didn't seem so awful.

'We're at the base of the ramp leading into the tunnel,' she said. 'I can see the door.'

'Hold on for a minute,' Ros told her. Pukje was already moving, scampering up through the web and into the rafters. 'There's bound to be a charm on the tunnel entrance, just like there is here. As soon as you step through it, the Scarecrow and Quirk will know.'

'So how are we going to get in?'

'Pukje's on his way down to pick the lock. He's coming the roundabout way, but he shouldn't be long. When you see the door open, go through as fast as you can and then separate.'

'But the charm —'

'Don't worry about it. We want it to go off.'

'Ah.' Distantly, through his mind's eye, he saw her nod. 'We're a distraction.'

'Exactly. It's the best way we can think of to divide Quirk and the Scarecrow. If Manton and Bronhill go in one direction while you and Know-it-All head in another —'

'They won't know who to chase. Oh, nice.'

Ros quickly filled in his role in the plan while they waited for Pukje to arrive. The Scarecrow would know where he was at all times. The trick would be to stay one step ahead of both it and Quirk at the same time.

Outside, the sunset daubed the restless sea with a wide palette of colours. Know-it-All stood knee-deep in the water, awaiting the command to proceed up the ramp. Adi sat astride him, while Manton stood at his right flank, absently patting his rump. Know-it-All didn't seem to mind, which gave Ros a pang of jealousy. The camel was normally wary of strangers, except those he took a particular liking to. Waiting on the cliff top had obviously given them time to bond.

Ros didn't immediately see Bronhill because the little man'kin was huddling inside the hood of Manton's travelling robe. Only her head was visible. She seemed terrified of the water, which Ros could understand. If she slipped and fell, she would sink straight to the ooze on the bottom and never find her way back to shore.

He withdrew to the door and saw Pukje already fiddling with the lock. The little man could move quickly when he had to. He was too small, however, to turn the heavy handle, so all he could do was give a thumbs-up once the door was unlocked.

'They can come in now?' Ros asked him through the Change.

Pukje nodded and scampered off.

Ros swept back to Adi to give her the news.

'Thanks, Ros,' she said aloud. 'Up we go, then.'

Splashing and dripping, the motley bunch exited the ocean and moved into the tunnel.

Anticipating an alarm, Ros glanced through the open door leading into the Scarecrow's laboratory. The machine-creature was working on its tangle of charms. The metal flower it used to drain things of the Change was much larger than it had been, now a cage easily big enough to fit an adult. It hung open like a wire mouth, ready to engulf its next victim. Ros shuddered on seeing it, and swore that it would never claim him.

Quirk was standing near the door, gnawing on a knuckle. He looked nervous and uncertain. His fingernails were bitten down to the quick. *Could he possibly be having second thoughts?* Ros wondered.

A high-pitched bell sounded, and both heads, human and machine, turned to face it.

'That's the door,' said Quirk with a look of concern. 'I know I locked it. The wind couldn't have blown it open.'

'Intruders?' the Scarecrow hissed.

Another bell sounded a different note.

'Someone is moving through the lower levels. Deal with them!'

Quirk hurried off to obey his master's orders. The Scarecrow reached for the tube lying on the nearest workbench and examined the red glow within.

That was Ros's cue. Opening his real eyes, he began moving upwards through the web to where he and Adi had entered it the previous day.

From far away, he heard the Scarecrow's cry of annoyance.

The chase was on.

He climbed up to the ledge at the base of the giant chamber's roof and made himself dusty all over again by slithering along it. There were several points at which he could have made his escape, but he chose one he had surveyed while waiting for Adi to arrive. It led into the warren of abandoned rooms the two of them had explored earlier. He would be hard to pin down in there.

Ros paused to catch his breath, wondering what Adi and the others were up to. He imagined Quirk running in circles, getting angrier by the minute.

From below and behind him came the sound of the Scarecrow's thudding footsteps. The web rang and shook as though gripped by a giant fist.

Ros scrambled into the shadows, confident that the thing would follow him wherever he went. That it couldn't fit onto the ledge wouldn't slow it down long. There were other ways up into the rafters, he was sure. The army that had once held the island would have made sure every position was defensible.

Into the decaying warren he headed. Night had fallen so there was little light, and he trod carefully over rotting floorboards and along crumbling walkways. Occasionally his way was lit by a section of the glowing cable, but the green glow cast no warmth and was much dimmer than it had been when they'd first arrived. He wondered how long the Scarecrow could survive on its meagre reserve. Weeks? Days? Hours?

From below came the sound of voices. Adi was taunting Quirk, daring him to find and catch her. Sometimes he could hear Know-it-All snorting and thundering along corridors meant for horses and cavalry. Quirk was keeping silent; he knew the corridors better than any of the intruders and presumably hoped to surprise them.

Ros imagined his master wanting to do much the same thing. The Scarecrow, however, was unable to move silently. Ros could hear it lumbering after him. Unsteady walls shook as it passed. Floorboards creaked.

Its labours gave Ros an idea. Looping around it, he headed for the route he, Adi and Varis had taken during their ill-fated escape attempt. The Scarecrow followed, growing more eager as he allowed it to come closer. Glancing behind him, he saw the light of its eyes through an opening in the wall. It shouldered through beams and piles of bricks, sending up clouds of dust.

Ros ducked through a rotting door and emerged onto a broad, flat rooftop. On the far side, a door hung invitingly open. He ran for it, trusting his memory and his feet to find the unbroken beam that crossed the floorless room within.

A flash of Varis almost falling crossed his mind like a lightning bolt. He felt the emptiness below him, yawning, sucking at him. His foot slipped in the dust on the beam and he gasped. Throwing himself forward, he put his faith in his hands and reached for the ledge on the far wall.

Behind him, the Scarecrow thundered through the door, taking half of the jamb with it. Its momentum was so great it was halfway into the room before gravity took hold of it. Its limbs whined as they flailed for the beams. Both planks of wood gave way under its weight, sending it tumbling down into the darkness. With a crash it went through the floor on the level below, then the one below that too, triggering an avalanche of debris.

Ros was hanging by his fingertips from the far ledge. He looked over his shoulder and saw, far below, a pair of green lights flickering on and off. He anxiously watched as one went out for good, then the other. All was dark and silent where the Scarecrow had fallen.

In far too precarious a position to enjoy his satisfaction, Ros grunted and hauled himself out of danger. With relief he hugged the dusty floor, catching his breath. The way back was closed to him now both beams were gone. He would have to press on and hope he could find another way to the laboratory. He could hear shouting and running coming from a different section of the island, so he had no fear of bumping into Quirk just yet.

He got up and dusted himself off, then moved quickly through the ruins until he had his bearings. Then he headed back to the web. From there he knew how to get to the laboratory, where the Scarecrow's foul machine awaited destruction.

When Ros reached the web, however, he slowed to a halt. Someone had got there ahead of him. A small figure crouched over Varis's body. The air was filled with the sound of weeping.

'Adi.'

She didn't look up as he approached her.

'Adi?'

Even when he was right behind her, she didn't look up. Her grief was impenetrable. She was hunched over Varis's chest. Dark hair hid her face. Bronhill was sitting on Varis's stomach, patting her gently.

'Hey, Jelena.'

She looked up at her heart-name and saw him hovering uncertainly nearby. 'Why didn't you tell me?' she said.

'I wanted to, but ...' He swallowed, afraid of her anger. 'But I didn't know how to.'

'What was so hard about it?' She climbed to her feet and came to stand in front of him. 'I don't understand.'

He wanted to explain, but again the words froze in his chest. Fighting the impulse to remain silent, he forced something out. 'I couldn't bring him back because I didn't know his heart-name. I was afraid you'd be angry.'

'Angry?' She half-laughed, half-sobbed, and wiped at her red eyes. 'I am angry, but not at you. I'm just glad to see you again. I'd begun to wonder if I ever would.'

To his surprise, she hugged him tightly, pressing her face into his chest and crying a little more. He held her, unable to find a better way to tell her that he was glad to see her too.

'I'm sorry,' he said into her hair.

'Me too,' she replied.

'No more secrets, I promise.'

'That's right,' she said, pulling away and looking down at Varis. Bronhill blinked up at them with stony eyes, puzzled by their behaviour. 'First you're going to tell me who did this, so I can get revenge.'

'I'm working on that right now,' he said, reminded of his mission. 'Come on.' He took her hand. 'I'll tell you on the way.'

She hesitated only to scoop up Bronhill, and then the three of them headed for the upper levels of the island fort.

* * *

They exchanged stories as they went. Adi explained how she and Manton had swapped companions halfway through the chase on realising that the upper levels were too cramped for the camel to enter. The last she had seen of them, he and Know-it-All were trailing Quirk from one side of the island to another. Eventually the Scarecrow's assistant would tire of it, but for now it seemed he was occupied. The echoes of the chase filled the corridors and halls. It sounded like a dozen people running back and forth, banging saucepans.

Ros told Adi about the Scarecrow's machine and Pukje's dire warning: they had to smash it to bits so it could never be used again.

'What about Escher?' she asked. 'Was he eaten?'

'No, Pukje's got him,' he said, hoping his mysterious ally was as good as his word. There had been no sign of Pukje since Adi had arrived. 'We'll deal with him after this, before anyone else gets any crazy ideas.'

'Are you sure that Scarecrow thing's dead?' she asked, following Ros up the second of three stairways leading to the spire.

'I'll show you where it fell after we've smashed the machine. You can poke it with a stick to make sure.'

'I'd rather drop rocks on it.'

Ros nodded. 'Big ones. Boulders.'

'I wonder if the bits would be worth anything,' she said, her eyes lighting up. 'Not to mention all these charms it's collected. This could be a real windfall for the Clan.'

140

'I can't believe you're thinking about money,' he said, stopping at the top of the last flight of stairs to catch his breath. 'I just want to go home.'

'To Mount Geheb?' Her gaze didn't leave him in the gloom.

He didn't have a ready answer for her. The word had come out before he'd really thought about it. Where was home for him now? With his family on the farm, or somewhere else?

There was only one answer that made sense to him.

'I mean the Clan,' he said.

She smiled. 'Well, you should talk to Father. I'm sure he'd let you stay with us, after this.'

'Didn't you say that I'd have to marry someone first?'

'Sure, but no one gets married before sixteen. Promised would be enough. After all you've done for us, I'm sure no one would object.'

He could feel a flush creeping up to his ears. 'But . . .'

'It could all be arranged when we get back. And it wouldn't change anything, really, except that everyone would know about it and you wouldn't have to leave. You could be one of us, a Sabatino, forever.'

'Wouldn't I . . . um . . .' Ros felt light-headed. One moment they were grieving for a dead friend and running from monsters. The next they were discussing the rest of his life in more detail than he had ever considered it before. 'Wouldn't I need someone to be promised to?'

She punched him in the arm. 'That's me, you idiot. Unless you've been making eyes at Aunt Radee.'

He didn't know whether to be relieved or terrified. 'Are you sure you want to? I mean, you were promised to someone when I first met you —'

'And see how well that worked out. Oh, Akil might have been all right, but I didn't know him. It wasn't my choice. I know you, Ros, and you won't see me trying to run away. Not if you promise to have a bath at the first available opportunity.'

Ros nodded, feeling very young and very grown up all at the same time. 'If it's your choice —'

'And yours too, of course.'

'— then ... I think ... okay.'

'Okay? Is that the best you can do?' She put her hands on her hips, but couldn't sustain her severe expression longer than a second. 'I know. This is crazy. We'll talk about it when we're off the island.'

He nodded. 'We will.'

'We've got plenty of time. It's good that you want to, though.'

Suddenly awkward, they stared at each other for a moment, still standing at the top of the stairs.

'Um, the laboratory is this way,' Ros said, indicating the enclosed walkway spiralling around the interior of the spire's walls. 'We're almost there.'

'And then it'll finally be over,' she said, walking beside him as the path began to ascend. 'Are you going to set it on fire or just smash it to bits?'

'I don't know yet. It might still be protected. Maybe Pukje can help. I'll call him.'

Ros cast his mind outward as they followed the curving wall, their footsteps crunching on the stone floor. Pukje wasn't easy to find. Ros spotted Manton and Know-it-All first, and a weary-looking Quirk. It wasn't until they reached the entrance to the laboratory that he located Pukje perched high above them.

'What are you doing up there?' Ros asked, leading Adi into the laboratory's cluttered tangle of charms and workbenches. 'Why aren't you down here with us?'

Then he noticed the trail of rubble leading through the doorway and the detritus their feet had been crunching on as they walked. Pukje, hearing Ros's mental voice, pointed urgently, but the intricate pile of machinery leaning against the wall behind them was already moving. Metal, leather and wood creaked as two limbs reached. With a hiss of steam, two green eyes flickered into life.

'Foolish boy-thing,' screeched the Scarecrow, clutching Ros and Adi about their throats in a scissor-grip too tight to escape. 'Treacherous, cunning and deceitful. You would steal my secrets, but I have you now! This time you will not escape.'

No matter how hard Ros wrenched at the mechanical arm he couldn't break away. The Scarecrow's casing and limbs were battered and bent by the fall, but it was whole enough to make good on its threat. With shuddering steps, it heaved its two prisoners towards the waiting cage.

'No!' gasped Ros, kicking and struggling. 'You can't do this!'

'I can do anything I desire.'

Adi was fighting just as hard. 'Burn it, Ros! Do something!'

Ros conjured up the charm he had used to set Kuller on fire and directed it at the machine waiting on the far side of the room.

Barely had the tangle of charms begun to glow when the Scarecrow stopped and swung Ros around to face it. Adi remained outstretched, making choking noises.

'Burn my handiwork,' the Scarecrow hissed, 'and I snap the girl-thing's neck.'

Ros wriggled and pulled, but there was nothing he could do. In desperation, he dropped that charm and tried another.

'Help!' he cried out to Manton and Pukje through the Change. 'We need help!'

Nothing came from above, but Manton heard and changed tack. Instead of tormenting Quirk, he headed upwards, to the source of the call.

Satisfied that its threat had had the required effect, the Scarecrow resumed dragging Ros to the wire cage. Its innards grated and whined, running on the last dregs of the Change.

Ros cursed himself for not coming straight to the laboratory. If he hadn't delayed by talking to Adi, the Scarecrow wouldn't have had time to heave itself up to its workshop and lie in wait for him. The tube monitoring Ros's movements was on the workbench by the door. The Scarecrow had known exactly when he had been about to arrive, when to hide in readiness for him.

Bronhill climbed off Adi's back and scampered along the Scarecrow's arm. Furiously but impotently she bashed her tiny fists against the Scarecrow's dented skull.

'Go for the eyes,' Adi told her. 'Blind it!'

The Scarecrow snarled as Bronhill reached into its eye sockets and tore at the delicate wires and gears within. Ros staggered, surprised, as the Scarecrow let go of him to brush the man'kin away. But before he could regain his footing, a solid metal fist struck him between the eyes and stars exploded inside his skull.

He barely heard Adi shouting as the Scarecrow dragged him to the wire cage and hauled him over its sharp lip. A deeper voice joined Adi's; Manton had arrived, but he too could do nothing while the Scarecrow had Adi in its grip. Ros stirred weakly, trying to prevent the lid closing over him. There was a brief tussle between him, Adi and the Scarecrow, but in the end the machine proved too strong.

The lid closed. Ros was trapped.

The Scarecrow didn't waste any time. It crossed to the bank of switches and pulled several in a sequence. The machine groaned into life. A wave of the Change passed through Ros, restoring him to full alertness — far too late. He was inside the machine. It was switched on and building power. The cage was charmed shut and he didn't have the first idea how to get out. The Scarecrow was peering in at him with hungry anticipation.

In desperation, Ros reached out with his mind to Pukje.

'What do I do?' he asked.

The little man mouthed one word: *Remember*.

'Remember what?'

The ocean.

A ghastly feeling blossomed in Ros's gut. He curled into a ball, clutching his stomach. It was the machine, sucking the life out of him, sucking him inside out. The Scarecrow's masterwork was killing him the same way it had killed Varis.

Every cell in his body cried out in pain as the Change began to leach from him.

Outside, sparks flashed and balls of bright green light played backwards and forwards along the cable. Shadows danced crazily across the faces of Adi and Manton — and Quirk, now standing in the doorway. He must have followed Manton to the laboratory, Ros guessed in a distracted way. Everyone seemed to be moving in slow motion.

His own life was slowing down as the last of his seconds passed by. It had been a better life than he sometimes appreciated. He had come such a long way from the family farm in such a short time, and there was much that he would miss when it ended. For all the ugliness and pain, there was beauty and joy too. He felt sorry for his sister, who would never see half as much as he had, even if she lived five times as long. She wouldn't even know what she was missing.

But that was little consolation for dying.

Ros's journey had started in a drought and would — unless he thought of something quickly — end on the edge of a world-full of water.

The suction of the Change from his flesh made him think of the ebbing tide, and that in turn reminded him of what Pukje had told him.

The ocean.

Feverishly, he wondered what that might mean. How could the sea possibly help him now?

Then he remembered how Pukje had taught him to break out of the cage — by taking the natural Change flowing through the ocean and channelling it into the containment charm.

That was it. That was what Pukje had meant. The machine was draining him like a person drinking a glass of water. Once that glass was empty there would be nothing left of him. But if he could connect the ocean to the glass, the machine could suck forever and he would never go dry.

Time had almost stopped around him. When he reached for the ocean, it was distant and dark, like a memory of babyhood. It slipped through his fingers, as insubstantial as steam. He tried again, knowing it was his last chance, goaded on by the sight of Adi straining to free herself from her captor's metal grip, tears shining like stars on her cheeks. The ocean didn't want to be grasped. It wasn't bedrock, stone to be held and pulled closer. It had to be lured, drawn in, breathed ...

With a thunderous boom like a wave crashing over him, the ocean's full force rushed in and time started again.

The green cable was glowing brightly. With a pleased hiss, the Scarecrow pushed Adi away and reached for one of the glowing threads and slipped it into its abdominal workings. Its eyes flared with new vigour, and when Manton rushed it, it batted him aside as though he were a child.

'Yes,' it roared. 'Yes!'

'Ros?' Adi was as close to the cage as the heat would let her. She tried to open it, but couldn't without burning herself. 'Ros, can you hear me?'

He realised that he was staring dumbly at her. His lips wouldn't move. His brain wouldn't work. His muscles were shaking like an old man's. Everything he sucked out of the sea, the machine absorbed, making him a channel through which powerful forces were flowing. The torrent overwhelmed him, consumed him.

Behind Adi, the machine was glowing like molten gold and smoking with heat. Quirk wrung his hands anxiously.

The Scarecrow seemed to grow in size as waves of energy flowed into it. Its metal plates swelled. Wooden joints creaked. Leather sinews strained to breaking point.

'Yes! So much power!' it bellowed.

Lightning flashed again. Claps of thunder drowned all thought. The glowing cable seared into Ros's vision, as bright as the sun.

At the other end of the channel, he felt the waves grow still and the sea flatten like glass all around the island. Currents stalled. Fish expired mid-gasp. If the machine wasn't stopped, the life-giving flow of the ocean might die forever.

But it's me doing this, Ros thought. *I'm killing part of the world in order to save myself. Isn't that just what the Scarecrow's doing?*

He raised the last dregs of his will to disconnect the machine from the ocean. He would rather die than become the thing he had tried to destroy.

The moment the current from the sea ceased, the machine began drawing from him again, and he had only so much left to give.

Then a small shape dropped from the ceiling, landing

near where Bronhill had fallen. Shaking the tiny man'kin awake, Pukje pointed at the machine and spoke rapidly into her ear. She nodded and scurried across the room, towards the glowing charms. Where flesh had failed, stone fingers would prevail. Lightning bolts crackled across the room as she threw herself bodily into the sabotage.

The machine faltered. Ros shuddered. The Scarecrow wheeled about in alarm. Wild surges of the Change flowed backwards and forwards through them both. Green light flared.

With a groan, the machine stopped working.

Into the ringing emptiness, the Scarecrow said, 'No matter.' Its eyes burned like fire. Sparks snapped and crackled from its fingers and joints. So much energy coursed through its body that every part of it quivered. 'I have all I need, for now.'

With one sweeping glance it took in the room: Ros helpless in the cage; Adi futilely imploring him to answer her; Bronhill struggling from the molten wreckage of the charms; Manton gripping an iron bar but not knowing what to hit with it; and Pukje, crouched on one knee on a workbench, watching with a thoughtful eye.

The Scarecrow took two thudding steps towards the little man. 'You, my enemy, cannot defeat me now. Long have you circled this stronghold, hungering for its maker's secrets. I will fix the machine and drain you next.'

With unbelievable speed, it lunged for him. Pukje only just managed to leap away in time. Glass retorts and delicate tools scattered in his wake. The Scarecrow pursued him, pushing benches aside as though they were made of paper.

'Dance all you want. I am indefatigable. With the energy harvested from the boy-thing, I could chase you a thousand years and never grow weary.' The glowing string trailed behind it, still connected to the cable that contained all the energy of the sea. 'I will pin you like a bug while I repair the damage you caused; and when I have done that, I will drain you too. Then the stone pest, then —'

'Master?' Quirk had moved into the room. His eyes were sunken. His hands hung at his sides, shaking. 'Master, the boy. He lives.'

Ros had struggled to a sitting position. His head ached as though hammers were pounding it. Despite all the strength of the Change that had flowed through him, he had none left for himself.

The Scarecrow knew it. 'The boy is drained. He cannot harm me, and neither is he of any use to me. Kill him, Quirk. Throw his body out with the garbage.'

Adi put herself between Quirk and the cage. 'Don't you dare touch him.'

'Master . . .'

'What's wrong, Quirk? This is no time to be squeamish. Kill her too, if she stands in your way.'

Quirk was frozen. Ros could see the conflict in his eyes. For years he had served his machine-like master, buying charms so it could live. Then had come the plan to take a golem and drain it of life — and what harm was there in that? Golems were evil by definition. They didn't deserve to live.

But now Varis had been killed, and Ros and Adi were threatened. Where would it end? How long until the Scarecrow decided it didn't need an assistant any more and fed him into the machine too?

Indecision twisted Quirk's face into an agonised mask. His feet were frozen to the floor.

'My maker never suffered such incompetence.' The Scarecrow hissed with annoyance. 'Must I do everything myself?'

Turning its back on Pukje, it strode to the cage and towered over Adi. She stood her ground bravely, even as its clawed right hand swept up over her head, deadly and powerful.

Ros gripped the cage and shook it, heedless of the burning metal. It couldn't end like this. It couldn't!

Quirk rushed forward. At first Ros thought he was going to throw himself between Adi and his master, to take the blow that would kill her, but his objective was the bank of switches controlling the Scarecrow's reservoir of the Change. He struck them with both palms, flipping them all down at once.

Emitting an ear-piercing howl, every iota of energy stored in the glowing cable rushed into the Scarecrow's body.

For an instant, the creature endured. Power filled every part of it, making it blaze with a sickening light. Green was the colour of living things, of grass and leaf, but life wasn't always pleasant — Ros could attest to that. Living things grew sick and died, rotted, were murdered before their time, *ended*. Death was part of life too, and the colour that blazed from the Scarecrow's eyes was purely morbid.

It swelled up, bones snapping and sinews tearing. The hard plates defining its chest and skull glowed and steamed and stretched. Force of will held it together, nothing more. The sound of its exertion was a rising howl. Stone crunched to dust beneath it. Its head brushed the ceiling. Its eyes burned like the sun. 'See how I have grown?' it roared.

Then it exploded.

Thousands of pieces — cogs, bolts and tiny jewels — blew outwards in a rush, knocking over benches and smashing charms. Everyone was blown off their feet — except Ros, who was tossed inside the cage like a die in a cup. Fragments of burning wood filled the air. Droplets of molten metal burned their skin. The terrible explosion drowned out all other sound.

Ros's senses were momentarily overwhelmed. When they returned, he was on his hands and knees, coughing. The cage had split open, and he crawled free of it, looking for Adi. The room was full of smoke. There was no light at all. All trace of green had vanished.

A flame sputtered into life. Pukje had lit a piece of paper from the smouldering wreckage. Quickly, he transferred the flame to a length of wood, which he raised to survey the damage. Pale faces approached out of the ruined laboratory's gloom: stunned Manton, blinking Bronhill, and Adi. When she caught sight of Ros, she ran to him and helped him to his feet. Her hands didn't let go of him when he was standing, and he was glad as ever for the comfort and strength they gave him.

'Is it over?' she asked.

Ros couldn't answer. His voice had left him, as it always did when he pushed the Change too hard. It would return once he had properly reconnected with the world.

Pukje, too, said nothing. Instead, he skipped over the rubble with his flame held high, searching until he found Quirk. The man lay on his back with one arm thrown across his face. When Pukje moved his arm, they saw a horrible thing: a fragment of the Scarecrow protruding from his right eye socket. The fragment had killed him, even as Quirk had killed his master. Their fates had been entwined.

'I'd say that's the end of it,' Pukje said, covering the fatal wound.

'Good,' Adi said, squeezing Ros's hand tightly. 'Forget about the money,' she said to him. 'I just want to get moving. All of us — including Varis.'

Manton snapped out of his daze. 'Oska!' he cried, rushing to the door.

'Who?' Adi called after him.

'The camel,' he yelled back. 'That's his name!'

With that mysterious comment he was gone. Bronhill scampered after him.

Ros felt his knees beginning to shake.

Adi led him to an overturned bench, where he could rest his weight. 'It's okay,' she said. 'There's no hurry. We can wait here until you're feeling stronger.'

Ros nodded, thinking of the journey ahead: back to the beach, up the cliffs, along the road to Samimi. Then finding Tally Wiskins so Adi could carry out her trade for the Clan, restoring the normality they dreamed of.

'Here,' said Pukje, climbing up to stand next to him. The little man pressed something into his hand. 'You might want this.'

It was the Scarecrow's charmed tube, which it would have used to track Ros wherever he went. It was dusty and battered but the red glow burned on.

'And this. I told you I'd keep it safe.'

The second object was the crystal. Escher. Flames danced across its quartz face as Ros held it lightly in one palm. It weighed almost nothing, but somehow it dragged at him, like everything he was afraid of condensed into one small object.

A treacherous voice whispered in his mind: *You'll never be free of it.*

He closed his fingers over the crystal, silencing the voice. It didn't come from Escher. It came from himself, and he wouldn't listen to it. He would get rid of this burden. He would live the life he wanted. No matter how long the road was, he would follow it to the end, one step at a time.

Finding strength from somewhere, he stood and took Adi's hand.

'Let's go,' he said, and together they put the ruined laboratory behind them.

8

Sweet Sorrow

Shortly after dawn the following morning, Ros was flying on the back of a dragon. It wasn't the strangest thing to have happened to him in recent days, but it was certainly one of the most memorable. From hooked nose to tail, the dragon stretched six metres long, and its powerful wings spanned almost twice that. Muscles flexed rhythmically beneath him, maintaining a steady beat.

The view was spectacular. They were so high up Ros couldn't see the waves on the surface of the sea, and the coastline behind him was barely a brown haze on the horizon. Despite this, he had actually nodded off a couple of times. There hadn't been time to sleep more than an hour or two since leaving the island. Lying face forward against the dragon's warm back, it was easy to let himself drift away.

Perhaps sensing that Ros wasn't an entirely attentive passenger, the dragon chose that moment to strike up a conversation. A voice rumbled from deep in its chest, perfectly audible over the wind.

'What was that all about back there, between you and Manton?'

Ros roused himself. 'I thought you saw everything.'

'I was busy out in the scrub, if you'll recall.'

Ros did, now he was prompted to.

'Did you never wonder why Manton was helping us?' he said, but didn't wait for an answer. 'We first saw him at the inn in Samimi, where we were all staying. Quirk was telling the stories about me. Manton got up in the middle and walked out, saying the stories were lies. Then Varis found him hanging around the stables and scared him off. The next morning, he helped us get away after Varis had been taken, and it never made sense why he would go to so much trouble.'

'It wasn't out of the goodness of his heart?'

Ros shook his head and sat up a little straighter. 'It was because of Know-it-All. The part of Quirk's story Manton didn't like was about me winning the camel from a trader in a contest — because *he* was that trader, and he knew as well as I did that I stole Know-it-All from him. I stole his pack too, leaving him stranded in the middle of nowhere. I never learned his name, but Manton never forgot mine. As if me taking all his stuff wasn't bad enough, people were saying that I was smarter than him. It must've made him wild.

'He got home to Samimi somehow, and the stories followed him there. That night in the inn, after he stormed out, he realised that Quirk was telling the story to get a reaction out of us. He checked the stables: there was a camel, and he did look a lot like Know-it-All — or Oska as he used to be called. But the sand bandits had branded Know-it-All, and that made Manton wonder if he was just being paranoid. Then Varis came and sent him packing and he went to bed.

'The next day, when I woke everyone up, Adi and I were going on about Varis being missing, and Manton thought we were talking about Know-it-All. The camel was still there, though, and that was when it all fell into place. Manton's smarter than Quirk, and he was closer to the truth of the stories. He guessed that one of us must be Roslin of Geheb, and that Quirk had kidnapped the wrong guy. When Adi and I headed off to rescue Varis, he came with us, because he was worried about Know-it-All. He didn't want his old friend getting caught in the middle of something dangerous. That's why he helped us.

'When Adi and I decided to sneak onto the island, Manton agreed to stay behind to look after Leda and his camel. He promised not to run away because by then he'd worked out that Know-it-All wasn't a prisoner. Still, he must have thought more than once about stealing Know-it-All back. He had the chance. I'm glad he didn't take it.'

'Does he still want Know-it-All back?' the dragon asked.

'Camels choose their own masters, he says. I think that means it's not up to either of us.'

A deep rumbling noise came from the dragon's chest. It sounded like laughter.

They flew in silence for a while. Ros let the wind whip his curly hair back and forth. It wasn't an unpleasant feeling. The horizon ahead was perfectly flat and featureless, like a desert but blue.

'You know,' Ros said, 'I impersonated Manton once. Before I went back home. I pretended to be him in order to fool Kuller. It worked too. But I didn't recognise him when I met him.'

'That happens sometimes. You'd met me before too. In a sense.'

'No. I'd remember that for sure!'

'The night in the inn when Quirk knocked everyone out,' the dragon said, 'do you remember dreaming?'

Ros cast his mind back. 'I do,' he said. 'Someone was calling my name, but I couldn't answer.'

'That was Quirk doing the calling. He was trying to make you reveal yourself. Varis got up to check the stables again, and that was where Quirk became confused.'

'So why didn't I answer him? What stopped his charm from working?'

'Me,' said the dragon. 'That's when our minds first touched. I was already following you then. And Quirk too. The last thing I wanted was for him to get his hands on the golem.'

Ros struggled to piece it all together. 'But you helped us get onto the island. And you didn't tell us what was going on there — we'd have been more careful if you had. Why would you do that if you didn't want the Scarecrow to become more powerful?'

'I knew nothing I said would turn you back. It would be better, I thought, to give up fighting the inevitable and instead show you how to fix it yourself. Give a man a fish and so on.'

'What fish?'

'Give a man a fish and he eats for a day; teach him

how to fish and he eats forever. You don't know that saying? It's been around almost as long as people have been catching fish.'

Ros hadn't heard it before, but that wasn't surprising. Until just days ago, he'd never seen a body of water larger than a rusting rain tank.

The dragon's wings flapped once more then became rigid, embracing the wind like an eagle waiting for prey. They glided, losing height, long enough for Ros to wonder if something had gone wrong. The thought of being stranded so far out to sea was spine-chilling. He'd have no hope of getting back to shore.

'I think this will do,' the dragon told him. 'See how the water is darker here? That means it's nice and deep. Just what you need.'

Ros's breath hitched in his throat. He reached with his right hand for the pouch at his side and clutched it tight. Now that the moment was upon him, he found it surprisingly hard to get on with it.

'Are you sure I'm doing the right thing, Pukje?'

'Absolutely,' the dragon replied. 'Don't take too long saying goodbye, though. We've still got a way to go and my wings are getting tired.'

Ros nodded. His fingers were numb as he took the crystal out of its pouch and held it up to the light.

The realisation that the dragon and the little man were one and the same had crept up on Ros slowly. It wasn't until they were resting at the top of the cliff after their long ascent that he'd asked Pukje the question that had been nagging him for some time.

'You and the dragon,' he'd said, 'are you working together?'

'Not exactly,' Pukje had replied. 'Our arrangement is a little more unusual than that.'

'How?'

'Would you like to ask it that question?'

Ros had looked around and up, half-expecting to see the creature's broad wings blocking the stars above them. 'It can talk?'

'When it wants to.'

'What are you two going on about?' Adi said.

Ros had gone over the clues for her: the hint that Pukje had dropped about seeing them at the cemetery; the Scarecrow's use of the word 'enemy' to describe both Pukje and the dragon; the way the dragon had tried to rescue him from the ocean; Pukje's ability to move around the island's highest vantage points with astonishing speed. They all made sense if Pukje had a flying steed to help him get around.

'Then why wouldn't he tell us about it?' Adi asked. 'Why keep something like that secret?'

They both looked around to ask Pukje, but he was nowhere to be found.

'He's not the only one with a secret,' Manton had said, and went on to reveal his past relationship with Know-it-All, to Ros's wonderment and unease. The camel had been stolen, yes, but Ros had tried to set him free before confronting the golem. When Know-it-All had turned up later, to carry him in pursuit of Adi's family, he had known then that he had earned one ally he could rely on completely.

The familiarity with which Know-it-All related to Manton, and the concern that Manton had showed him, made sense to Ros then. He could only imagine how it would have felt to lose Know-it-All to a thief, to worry about how the camel was being treated, then to hear that some young would-be hero was dragging him off on adventures no mere trader could offer.

But Manton didn't seem angry about what had happened in Barker, although it was clear from the way he spoke that he had been, once. Now he seemed more mystified than anything — by the way fate had conspired to bring them together, and how events had played out in the previous days.

'This is as confusing for me as it is for you,' he'd told them at the Coach and Camel, shortly before advising them not to thank him for his help until they knew the reason he was helping them.

Well, now Ros knew, and he was still grateful. Manton was an honourable man — more honourable than Ros had initially given him credit for being. And Ros felt bad for having caused him so much trouble. If only some of Manton's good nature had infected him when he had tried to impersonate him on the road to Mount Geheb!

'I used to think,' Manton said, 'that Oska was a perfectly good name, but that was before you showed me otherwise. Know-it-All suits him much better. Sometimes I think he understands every word I say.'

The camel had huffed softly in the moonlit gloom. They had made a temporary camp near the tree line and lit a small fire to keep the night's chill at bay. Know-it-All was sitting behind Adi, occasionally regarding them all with a dark-eyed indifferent gaze. He didn't seem perturbed by recent events, nor particularly relieved to see Ros again.

'I reckon he's enjoying this immensely,' Adi had said. 'All that running around on the island — he probably hasn't had so much fun for years.'

Manton laughed. 'I think you're right. And he's welcome to it. If half of what they say about Ros is true — and I'm beginning to suspect it is — you've done more than most people in a lifetime.'

'There's much more to come,' rumbled a voice from the shadows, 'if he can keep himself out of trouble long enough to find the right teacher.'

They had jumped to their feet as an enormous shape stepped up to the fire. Like a giant bird but with grey-green skin, it had a beaked nose and clawed feet, and its immense wings were folded flush against its back. The firelight danced in its eyes, which looked amused at their fright.

'Once upon a time,' the dragon said, 'the world was full of creatures like me. We are rare now, and for the most part we avoid your kind. We see the fear in your eyes when you gaze upon us. It's unpleasant, for we belong in this world as surely as you do. It was ours before it was yours. We understand it a little better. So we hide ourselves in a variety of different ways. Some of us live in the sky, as clouds or mysterious lights. Some live underground, feasting on molten rock. Some spread their wings in the canopies of forests, where vines will hide them and they can sleep out the rest of eternity.

Some find ways to walk among you, as I do, as one of you. It is difficult, but it can be done.'

Something about the voice and the way the dragon was watching him made Ros realise the truth. 'Are you ... can you really be ... Pukje?'

The great winged beast nodded. 'I went into the bushes to change. I can't do it when people are watching.'

The camel huffed again, unimpressed. Know-it-All was the only one of them that hadn't reacted with surprise.

Ros stepped close enough to touch the dragon. It ... *he* radiated heat like a furnace. 'Why didn't you tell us earlier?' he said.

One giant eye fixed on him. 'I didn't think you needed to know. The Scarecrow and I disagreed on a lot of things, Ros, but when it comes to you we thought exactly the same. Get rid of the golem first; help you find your potential second. I'm not saying the Scarecrow wasn't being selfish when it offered to teach you what it knew; I'm certainly not saying I won't be the same. But I will tell you this: at dawn tomorrow we're flying from here to drop that crystal into the deepest ocean trench I can find. Only then will you be free to talk about what comes afterwards.'

Ros had wished he could run away. Everyone was looking at him. Even Bronhill had stirred from Manton's pack and was watching him with wide, solemn eyes. The air seemed to grow solid around that moment, as it had in the Scarecrow's lab an instant before the machine would have killed him. *In moments like these*, he'd thought, *lives change forever.*

'All right,' he'd said. 'Dawn tomorrow. You'll wake us?'

'Don't make me shake you twice,' Pukje had said, grinning enormously. 'My bite is much worse than my bark.'

Ros had pretended to be unconcerned while unfolding his pack and lying down next to Know-it-All to sleep, but secretly his heart was unsettled by the sudden development. Tomorrow was very soon, much sooner than he had expected. Finding a boat and a sailor he could trust to ferry them safely out into the ocean and back could have taken days. Weeks, even.

Only when Adi lay down next to him, giving him her warmth as well, had he finally begun to relax. And as soon as he did that, the exertions of the previous days took their toll. He was asleep in a moment, and he didn't dream.

And now, hours later, he and Pukje were practically skimming the wave-tops, waiting for him to make good on his promise.

Holding the object of his confusion in his hand only made his uncertainty worse. Apart from a single fracture deep in its depths, the quartz crystal was featureless. There was no evidence of the creature trapped within, and for one crazy moment Ros wondered if it really was just a stone he had picked up on the farm one day. The notion that within this tiny thing, barely as large as his thumb, rested one of the most hate-filled minds that had ever bothered humanity was, well, absurd.

'Sherec,' he said, speaking the true name he had given the Golem of Omus. 'Can you hear me?'

Something stirred in the stone. He felt it not through his skin, but through the Change. Something was alive in there. That something was listening.

'Goodbye,' he said.

With a single, impulsive motion, he thrust his right arm away from him. The crystal tumbled from his palm and spun end over end towards the waves. The sun caught it as it fell. One bright gleam struck his eye like a rebuke, making him blink.

Then it was gone, vanished into the deep water where the light would never reach it again. Ros imagined it sinking for days until it struck the silty sea-bottom, to be embraced by ooze for the rest of eternity.

He waited for relief, gladness and joy to bloom within him.

But he felt no different at all.

He was still heavy, even with the burden of the golem expelled. He was still tired. He was still anxious about what lay ahead of him. He still had so many questions.

'Who were you following first?' he asked Pukje as the dragon turned and began the long flight back to the shore. 'Me or Quirk?'

'You.'

'Why?'

'Because you're different.'

'Different how?'

'The Change can be encouraged, guided and nurtured, but it doesn't come to just anyone. Usually

Stone Mages breed more Stone Mages, and the same goes for Sky Wardens. It's not often that someone new and fresh comes along to shake everyone up. I take it as a positive sign.'

'So you heard the stories too?'

'Yes, and tracked you down to see if they were true. They were. From then, I only had to be patient. It was just a matter of time before you came to someone else's attention.'

'The Scarecrow.'

'Or any of a number of prickly personalities still making their way in the world. I have made quite a few enemies who would love to make your acquaintance. Until you learn to contain it, your light will draw all manner of things your way.'

Ros considered that with a heavy heart. He remembered Mage Shurven saying that he shone, and that was what had drawn the Golem of Omus to him. The dust devils had come too, and now the Scarecrow and Pukje had also found him irresistible.

'How do I stop it?' he asked.

'Through careful study and application,' Pukje replied, 'like all things worth achieving.'

'That's why I need a teacher, then. To stop being so obvious about using the Change.'

'Exactly. You're figuring things out pretty well on your own, but the way you're going you'd be lucky to last another year. Someone or something will eventually take you by surprise, along with anyone close to you, and that'll be the end of it.'

The dragon banked slightly to the left, then resumed

its steady flight. 'Has no one ever told you that before?' it asked him.

'No.'

'Well, I have now, and I hope you'll listen.'

Ros thought of Varis, and Adi in the Scarecrow's tightening grip. The dead Clansman had been wrapped in a makeshift shroud and would receive the proper funeral rites in Samimi, but that was the best they could offer him. They couldn't bring him back; they couldn't undo the pain and suffering he had experienced; they couldn't undo the grief his family would feel.

Ros would never forget the wonder he had felt when Escher had taught him his first charm. Little had he known then how that tiny flame would spread to engulf his entire world. He was beginning to realise that Adi's dream of being a trader might be infinitely preferable to a life filled with the Change and the perils that came with it.

'Will you teach me, Pukje?'

'What was that? I can barely hear you.'

Ros repeated the question in a louder voice. 'Will you show me how to live like this without hurting anyone?'

'I can try, and I'd be happy to. But there are two conditions.'

Ros bit down on an automatic refusal. 'What are they?'

'Well, as you know, I never do anything for nothing. If I help you, it'll be because I expect something in return. This time, I don't know what that something might be. It could be a favour, a gift, a lesson of your own perhaps — and of course I won't force you to do anything you don't want to do. But that would be my first condition: when I've taught you everything I can, you'll owe me something substantial, of my choosing, before we go our separate ways.'

That didn't sound too onerous, Ros thought. He was under no illusions that the education he needed would come without cost of some kind, and if he couldn't be forced into doing something he didn't want to, what harm could there possibly be?

'I'll think about it,' he said. 'Tell me the second condition.'

'This kind of training can be dangerous. We should begin as soon as possible — before your talents grow any wilder or something else takes a fancy to you — and we need to go about it in a safe place. I'd suggest leaving immediately, if I thought you'd agree to it —'

'Not before we get back to Samimi,' Ros said firmly. 'I have to help Adi find Tally Wiskins. I promised.'

'I know, so we'll wait that long but no longer. The second condition, Ros, is that when we leave, it's just the two of us. No one else.'

Ros unconsciously tightened his grip on Pukje's back. 'Why?'

'Well, I can only carry so many people, and there's the safety issue to think about. What if there's an accident? Or worse: what happens if we're discovered? Someone close to you might be used against you, and I know you don't want that. You need to be focused on the tasks I'm going to set, and you can't do that unless everyone else is well out of harm's way. That's why it has to be you and me, alone, for as long as it takes, or nothing.'

The dragon flew on for a dozen beats.

'It's up to you, Ros.'

Ros agonised in silence all the way back to the coast. This wasn't one of the possible futures he had imagined for himself. That he would be whisked across the world by himself and taught by a talking dragon seemed simultaneously too wonderful and too awful to be true.

How could he possibly accept? He had a life with the Clan waiting for him. He had promises to keep. But at the same time, how could he possibly turn it down? Did he really want to be a cook for the rest of his life, unable to use the Change for fear of someone else getting hurt?

Pukje didn't know everything. He had never claimed to, and Ros was sure of it now. Pukje was wrong on one very important point. The decision wasn't entirely up to Ros at all. There was one person he had to talk to first.

'You should agree to both conditions,' said Adi. 'You'd be an idiot not to.'

'Do you think so?'

'Don't you?'

'I'm not sure,' he said, feeling too downcast to be certain of anything. 'What if it takes years? What if we forget about each other? What if —'

He broke off, unable to put into words all the new fears he had. He had just got rid of the old ones. It wasn't fair that there should be so many to take their place!

Adi, perhaps sensing that talk would solve nothing for the moment, let silence have its turn.

Ros had asked for time alone with her as soon as he had arrived and, even though the animals were laden and ready to leave, she had seen the look on his face and agreed. They were sitting cross-legged at the cliff's edge, looking out over the ocean, a breeze that smelled of vast and watery expanses playing across them. Bulbous clouds drifted lazily overhead. Far below, breakers pounded stones painted white by seagulls. A tiny dot on the south-eastern horizon was probably a fishing boat, heading out empty in the hope of coming home full.

Adi was watching that dot too.

'Father has never seen the sea,' she said, 'but he used to tell me stories about it, of sailors and explorers and the far-off lands they supposedly visited. It used to drive my mother wild. The stories *she* told were always about how the world used to be — broken up into lots of little bits, she said, where now we have just one of everything. The big things, anyway. One sea, one coast, one land. That's why Father's stories made her so angry. There are no lands across the sea, she used to say, and dreaming of what isn't out there is dangerous. If we start chasing phantoms, she'd tell my father, we'll soon all be lost.'

'Am I a phantom to you?' Ros asked, thinking he had worked out what she was trying to tell him. 'I don't want you to get lost because of me.'

'I'd be dead if it wasn't for you,' she said matter-of-factly. 'I would've run off on my own and the crabblers would've got me. That's not what I'm saying at all.' She pressed her hands down on her knees. 'The old times must have been weird. I used to feel glad that I lived today, when nothing is broken up and everything is fixed.

But I think I know now what my mother was really angry about, even though she never said it. The world may look fixed, but it's not. Just having one of everything doesn't make life easy. People still argue. They still get sick and die. There's still confusion and choices and consequences. I guess that's what growing up is mostly about: realising that things stay broken sometimes, no matter how hard we try to put them back together.'

'But we still have to try, right?'

'Oh, yes, otherwise there'd be no point living. We just can't expect it to be easy all of the time.'

'I'd be happy with *some* of the time,' Ros said.

She smiled. 'Well, maybe you're getting all the hard stuff out of the way early. Maybe you'll just cruise along later.'

'Do you think so?'

'It's something to look forward to.'

Ros stretched his legs out in front of him. The distant boat was on the verge of invisibility. If he stared at it too hard it slipped out of sight and disappeared, but every time he looked away there it was again, dangling tantalisingly on the edge of his vision.

'I promise I'll come back to you,' he said.

'Well, I promise to wait.' She looked at him, shielding her dark eyes from the sun. 'Just don't die or anything and leave me waiting forever. That could be a little annoying.'

He smiled. 'I'll even try to write.'

'You'd better, but I guess I won't be able to write back, seeing Pukje wants to keep everything a secret. That doesn't seem fair.'

An idea occurred to him. 'I think I have a way to make it a little easier for you.'

'What's that?'

He climbed to his feet and held out his hand.

'No more secrets,' she said, quoting him.

'Can't you wait half a minute?'

'Why should I?'

'Easier to show you. Honest.'

They walked back to Know-it-All side by side, in perfect step. Pukje, returned to his impish, semi-human form, was far enough away to be out of earshot, and so were Manton and Bronhill. That the trader had a new companion to take the place of Know-it-All eased Ros's conscience somewhat, but it begged the question: what would Ros have done in his shoes? Would he behave so honourably if Know-it-All was ever stolen from him? Manton was the best possible example of how people should behave, but it took more than pretending to be him to inherit his strength of spirit. Ros wished it could be so easy.

Adi's jibe about secrets had reminded him of the one thing he hadn't told her yet. He still didn't want to tell her, but he had learnt the hard way that keeping it to himself would only come back to bite him later.

What would Manton do?

Slowing his pace, Ros confessed that it was Escher who had first given him her heart-name, in the crabbler caves, not Adi herself.

'Again, not a bad thing,' she said, 'because I would've died otherwise. But thanks for telling me. Is there anything else?'

'No,' he said, relieved it had gone so well.

'Good.'

'You?'

'You've read my mind. You know what's in there.'

'Not all of it.'

'Just the interesting bits.'

'I'm sure that's not true,' he said.

'Don't be. When you're not around, life tends to be pretty dull.'

They stopped at Know-it-All's side, and Ros reached into one of the saddlebags. His hand found the rod Pukje had given him in the ruined laboratory, and he produced it with a flourish.

'What's it for?' Adi asked.

'The Scarecrow made it,' he said. 'The light grows brighter when it points at me.'

Adi tested it out and was rewarded by a bright red glow. 'How far does it reach?'

'I don't know,' he said, 'but the Change is everywhere. I don't think distance really comes into it.'

She hefted it once, and Ros could see that her eyes were getting teary. This was the first concrete proof that they would be parting soon. He was struggling with it too.

'It's for me to keep?' she asked him.

'Yes. Wherever you're standing, you'll always know which direction I am.'

'Thanks, Ros. I think that'll help. If it ever goes out —'

'It won't,' he said.

'But if it ever does —'

'I promised I'd come back, and I will.'

She turned away to slip the rod into her pack. Her voice was muffled as she said, 'Manton has Bronhill now. I wonder if he'd let me look after Know-it-All for you, while you're gone.'

'It's not really up to him,' Ros started, but Know-it-All made his words unnecessary. Butting Ros aside, the camel pushed his long face against Adi's and snorted loudly.

Adi reached out to hug Know-it-All around his long, muscular neck. She was laughing and crying at the same time. Ros's cheeks were wet too, and for a long time the two of them stood together, arms entangled around Know-it-All, trying hard not to think about what lay ahead.

Again Ros thought of the riddle Yury had told him about the horizon. The sky and the sea never touched, but together they formed a perfect line. That was what he and Adi would be like when they were apart. He would hold true to that line, and he knew that she would too.

'The world isn't broken,' he said. 'Look at it. It's beautiful! There's grass and trees and birds, and a thousand things we can't even see right now. We could stay in this one spot for the rest of our lives and still not know everything about it. But there's so much stuff getting in the way. Life will be much better when that's all behind us.'

'Oh, I know that,' Adi said, her usual firmness restored to her voice. She wiped her eyes and blew her nose, and he knew she wouldn't cry again. 'How about that other promise you made — the one about finding

Tally Wiskins? I'm not letting you go until we've got the salt deal sorted, and the day's not getting any younger while we stand here gas-bagging.'

She whistled, piercingly loud, to attract the others. They came immediately, not seeming to mind that they'd been kept waiting.

Pukje climbed onto Ros's shoulder while Adi and Manton were checking that Varis's body was still firmly secured to the back of the mule they had rescued from the island.

'Have you decided?' the little man asked him.

'I have,' Ros said. 'The answer's yes.'

The only assurance he received from Pukje that he'd made the right choice was a brisk nod, but he supposed he didn't need more than that. Roslin of Geheb had fought dust devils and sand bandits, freed captives from the Bee Witch, and sent a golem to a watery fate. He could make the right decision when he had to.

They mounted up and headed off, and the sun shone brightly on their journey.

Where it all began ...

The Changeling

THE BROKEN LANDS: BOOK ONE

Ros is in real danger. His family are so desperate to save their drought-stricken farm that they'll sacrific anything — even him — for rain. His only friend is Escher, an unseen entity with a voice that whispers in Ros's head, continually warning him to leave before it's too late.

Escaping from his vengeful family astride a stolen camel. Ros decides to try his luck in the desert, discovering along the way a power he never knew he had. Through Escher, Ros learns to control the Change, a magical force that taps into the land, the water, fire and the air. He also meets Adi, a girl from a travelling clan of nomads, who asks him to save her from a future she's desperate to avoid.

When tragedy strikes, Ros seeks help from a powerful Stone Mage, but when even she can't save him, he starts to question everything that has happened on his journey. He must decide who is telling the truth, and who his real friends are.